Maresco Pearce

Philip of Königsmarkt and Poems

A Tragedy

Maresco Pearce

Philip of Königsmarkt and Poems
A Tragedy

ISBN/EAN: 9783743410084

Manufactured in Europe, USA, Canada, Australia, Japa

Cover: Foto ©Andreas Hilbeck / pixelio.de

Manufactured and distributed by brebook publishing software (www.brebook.com)

Maresco Pearce

Philip of Königsmarkt and Poems

Lately Publiſhed, price 5s., or with Plates on
India, 7s. 6d.

ILLUSTRATED WITH ETCHINGS BY

GEORGE CRUIKSHANK

THE

EE AND THE ASP

A FABLE IN VERSE

BASIL MONTAGU PICKERING

196 PICCADILLY LONDON W.

PHILIP OF KÖNIGSMARKT,

AND POEMS.

BY MARESCO PEARCE, B.A.

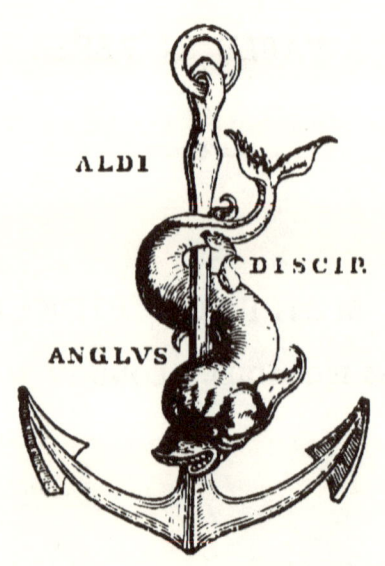

LONDON:

BASIL MONTAGU PICKERING,

196, PICCADILLY. W.

1863.

CONTENTS.

	PAGE
PHILIP of Königsmarkt. A Tragedy	1
SONNETS :—	
On the Beach, near Lyme Regis .	107
After Storm in Summer . .	109
" The child unquestioning treads his father's path"	111
The Alps, between Munich and Salzburg .	113
" The moon had risen in haste, and left her zone"	115
Farewell	116
Tears	124
" Come, dearest, for a while apart" . . .	127
Pure Love	130
Forbidden Love	132
The Puritan's Daughter . . .	136
The Last Night	188
The Maiden and the Lilies . . .	196
Love and Death	198
Song	200
The Portrait	201

	PAGE
Doubt	203
More Doubts	204
Old Love Letters	205
" As when a great oak dieth, that in life " .	206
Song in Sorrow	207
Love	211
Convent Thoughts	218
The Echo in the Baptistery of Pisa . . .	225
A Fragment	229
Horace. Second Epode	234
A Magdalen	242
The Artist's Child	245
The Starling	252
To the Memory of a Painter	254
Only	256
San Miniato	257
Margaret. A Retrospect	261
The Shrine by the Wayside	314
" The moon had left the throbbing sea " . .	322

PHILIP OF KÖNIGSMARKT.

A TRAGEDY.

B

DRAMATIS PERSONÆ.

Philip of Königsmarkt (*Colonel of Hanoverian Guards*).

Gustav, *his friend (Captain in ditto)*.

Elector of Hanover.

Crown Prince (*afterwards George I. of England*)

Guards, *among them two Italians in* Countess Platen's *pay*.

Courtiers.

Servant.

Sophie Dorothée, *wife of Crown Prince*.

Mary Dillon, *her favourite attendant*.

Countess Platen, *Mistress of the Elector*.

Maids of Honour.

PHILIP OF KÖNIGSMARKT.

A TRAGEDY.

ACT I.

Scene I.

A garden under the Princess's *Apartments, at night.* Enter Mary Dillon *and* Gustav *from opposite sides.*

Mary.

WELL, Signor Capitano, here you are at last; I got your letter, and admired your impudence in expecting me to stand out in the cold and damp for the sake of seeing you. And, pray, what brings you

and the Count back again to Hanover? No
good—I dare say.

GUSTAV.

Let me get my breath, and I'll answer as many
questions as you like to put.   But first, I must
thank you for coming to-night, though I knew
you would;—and then, O, what have we come
back for? Why we are tired of one kind of war,
and so are here to wage another.

MARY.

What, with an artillery of sighs and ogles, eh?

GUSTAV.

Yes, and one in which I don't know if we
shall triumph in the end, but we've got sadly
worsted at starting.

MARY.

Ah, that's one of your military manœuvres, to
draw the enemy from his intrenchments.   But
suppose the said enemy were to keep snug in his

(or her) stronghold, and decline to follow you, you'd cut but a sorry figure, I fancy.

GUSTAV.

Oh, she'll follow fast enough.

MARY.

Will she?

GUSTAV.

Why, Mary dear, if you knew anything of the code of honour, you'd be aware that in every duel, while the principals are engaged, the seconds get up a fight on their own account; and you must know that Mars and Venus have but one code of laws between them; so I mean to lay siege to your heart, while the Count—

MARY.

Hush! O my dear, kind, noble mistress! why has he come back to tempt her? I had almost rather that his great blue eyes were closed for ever than looking into—those that, alas, don't know how to frown at him; and his abominably handsome lips were—anywhere rather than so dangerously near hers—I wish I were in her place—

GUSTAV.

Do you?

MARY.

I'd teach my inferiors to respect me! and, if they dared to talk to me of love, I'd, I'd—

GUSTAV.

You'd, you'd bear it with equanimity, I dare say—for, look you, a Princess, after all, is but a woman, and it isn't being made love to that puts them out of temper. And supposing now that you were a princess, and that a presentable fellow, like myself, for example, were to give you a kiss like this—what would you do, eh? There's no law against it that *I* ever heard of. I'll ask my cousin, the councillor, whether there's any penalty for kissing a princess.

MARY.

Do try and be serious, and tell me what you know of this unhappy affair.

GUSTAV.

Know—well, all I *know* is that Philip, like me, is *really* in love ; *unlike* me though, it's not for the first time—for I swear by all that's solemn, that I never even *looked* on woman, till your loved image—

MARY.

There, that'll do, go on—

GUSTAV.

How *can* I go on, if you stop me in that way? I declare you've spoilt my pet speech that I composed as I came along. Well, I was going to observe that he really is in love, as am I, only that *I* never—

MARY.

Will you go on about the Count?

GUSTAV.

I will, I will—Well then we're both in love.
I'll make my meaning plainer by speaking in a
metaphor.   Our mouths water for two peaches,
that hang against a wall (I'm obliged to suppose
a wall); a good, ripe, rosy cheeked one, mine is,
bless it, and well within my reach.

MARY.

Don't make too sure.

GUSTAV.

Once for all, will you not interrupt me? Mine,
I repeat, is within my reach ; while his—(it's not
half so plump and juicy looking as mine, either)—
his is so high up, that he must make a tremendous
jump to get at it, and then he has a very good
chance of bringing the wall about his ears. You
see how well the *wall* comes in now.

MARY.

Oh, you men, you men ! All you think of is

the risk the Count runs,—and you forgot my dear lady, that is indeed a fruit so precious and delicate, that a touch might rub off the bloom and leave a mark. Who is he, that he should dare to look so high, and think to pluck such fruit?

GUSTAV.

Listen, there he is—I thought he wouldn't be long before he came.

[*The* COUNT PHILIP *is heard singing in the garden.*

SONG.

The night bird is singing in the brake, love,
　　To his mate in the nest;
And I will sing to thee till thou wake, love,
　　Till thou wake from thy rest.

The moon walketh on in starry mazes,
　　Like a queen among flowers;
These shall never fade away, like the daisies,
　　Nor shall love such as ours.

MARY.

Ah, he has a sweet voice, more's the pity.
I wish he had a quinzy.

GUSTAV.

Why if he had, she'd only come out all the
sooner to nurse him.   Do you think now, dear,
that a woman's love depends on a man's lungs?
Look how fond you are of me, and yet *I* never
sang you such pretty songs.

MARY.

No, that you certainly never did; hush!

SONG (*continued*).

Come forth, O belovèd, in thy glory,
  For the morn cometh soon;
Come forth among the trees that are hoary
  In the pale rays of the moon!

MARY.

Come forth! of course she will, poor thing.
Dear me, what fools we women are, to be sure.

SONG (*continued*).

The robins, love, are sleeping in the shadows,
  Each nest a dewy cup;
And the daisies, love, were sleeping in the
    meadows,
  Till the fairies woke them up;
But the jasmine at thy chamber ever keepeth
  Faithful watch through the night;
Breathing perfume to my darling, as she sleepeth,
  And sweet visions of delight.

GUSTAV.

Well, I never thought of talking about birds'
nests and jasmine, when I was courting; but
all ways in love seem to lead to the same end.

SONG (*continued*).

O that I were as the jasmine to clamber
  To her window there above,
I would woo her till she answer'd from her
    chamber,
  Till she answer'd to my love.

GUSTAV.

That's what he'll be doing presently, unless I'm very much mistaken.

MARY.

There, she's coming out into the balcony; we'll watch at the garden gate, and warn them in case of surprise; between ourselves, too, perhaps it's just as well we shouldn't see them.

GUSTAV.

Come along then, dear, I shall take a leaf out of the Count's book, and sing you such pretty songs about birds' nests and jasmine.—We've been courting on false principles all this time, I dare say; anyhow, there'll be no harm in beginning over again.

MARY.

Come along, and don't talk nonsense.

GUSTAV.

One kiss, and I will—

MARY.

There, that's enough,—now come along, do.

[*Exeunt.*

[*The* PRINCESS *in the balcony,* the COUNT
in the garden.

PRINCESS.

O Philip, am I sleeping or awake?

For your sweet voice so mingled with the dreams

I dream'd of you, that, when I half awoke,

And heard your song, I thought that still I slept;

And, when it ceased, I tried to sleep again,

To dream, and hear again.

COUNT.

Nay, my Princess,

This is no dream, but sweet reality;

I am no vision of your sleeping brain,

But your own Philip, come to whisper you

What you do know so well, yet love to hear,

How that I love you better than my life;

Nay, so much better, I would give my life,

To save you from a heart-ache.

PRINCESS.

But you know

How precious 'tis to me, and you shall keep it,

If only for my sake; but, Philip, dearest,

You must not stay, and yet I lack the words

To bid you go. It seems so very hard,

When I have wearied so to have you here,

That I must drive you from me; yet I must,

Not for your sake, but mine,—for should they
find you

Then would they kill you, and my heart should
die.

COUNT.

Nay, I will go; but ere I go, my queen,

Will climb into your balcony, and stay

A moment's space, and kiss the delicate hand

That shineth, like a lily, in the moon.

> [*He climbs into the balcony.*

PRINCESS.

O, Philip, what is this that you have done?

God! should they find you!

COUNT.

> Do you fear to die?

Look, dearest, if they find me we will die.

There is a subtle poison in this phial,

That kills if one but taste; this will I drink,

And you, my own, shall kiss my poison'd lips,

And drink the deadly moisture from my mouth,

And we will die together,—lips to lips.

But pale not, who should find me? do you think

Your burly lord would leave his painted mistress

To waste a thought on you?

PRINCESS.

> He is my husband.

COUNT.

Nay, my Princess, nay, he is *not* your husband;

Too true it is ye made a mutual compact

Before God's altar, to be man and wife;

But such holds good, so long as both respect

Their plighted troth; if one should break his vow

He frees the other, therefore you are free.

But, more than this, when we were little children,

And wander'd in the woods on summer eves,

I call'd you "little wife," and you me "husband;"

And, one day, you remember, I did fashion

A tiny ring out of a daisy stalk,

And put it on your finger; but it broke,

And you did cry, and I did kiss your tears.

Say was there ever purer love than this?

If ever love was heaven-born, was not ours?

And can this cursèd greed, and base ambition,

That gave you to another, part the souls

That God united? Heaven forbid it.

PRINCESS.

Philip,

There are two children here who call me

" Mother,"

And should I leave them, they would ask for me,

" Where is our mother?" and one should shake

his head,

As at a guilty thing we speak not of;

And they should blush, unknowing shame them-

selves,

My children for their mother's.   Pity me,

For I am very weak, and I do love you,

God knows how dearly, therefore pity me,

And leave me, Philip.

COUNT.

Fare you well, sweet lady,

I'll try to love you, as you would be loved;

I'll worship you; and you shall be to me,

As some fair image of a holy saint,

c

'Twere sacrilege to touch ; and guard the shrine,

That holds my idol, from the baser world ;—

Good-night.

PRINCESS.

Good-night.—O, Philip, now I think

I love you even better than before ;

God bless you for it, Philip, fare you well.

> [*He kisses her hand, descends from*
>
> *balcony, and exit.*

SCENE II.

COUNT PHILIP, *sitting on a bench in the park, is*
discovered by the COUNTESS PLATEN.

COUNTESS.

AN I believe my eyes ? can this be he,

The gay Count Philip, sitting here

alone,

Moody as " Melancholy " on the tomb

Of Medici at Florence? How is this?

Hath woman, then, presumed to frown at last?

Is it some silly girl who dares refuse

To *give* her heart for a brief loan of yours;

Or burgher's wife, who thinks a month of pleasure

Too dearly purchased at a life's remorse?

Or sit you thus, with brows that frown in thought,

Ripening some project, that shall hand your name

To latest days, the Conqueror of hearts?

Say, is it so, fair Count? or do you sigh,

Another Alexander, that the world

Hath nothing left to conquer?

COUNT.

Pardon me,

I do assure you, Madam, I was thinking—

I really forget what.—

COUNTESS.

I have it, Count—

You have been losing heavily of late.

Nay, do not shake your head.   The whole world
    knows it.
Believe me, you're too fortunate in love,
To hope for luck at cards.   You know the
    proverb ;
But, I have money—Do not frown at me—
I would not vex you—but you need not blush
To borrow of a friend—Sure better this
Than of some crafty and usurious Jew.

COUNT.

Madam, you do mistake me, I assure you ;
I have not lost beyond my power to pay,
And, if I had, I trust I'm not the man
To publish my vexation to the world.
But, pardon me, dear madam, if I leave you
Somewhat abruptly ; but it groweth late,
And I have an engagement—

COUNTESS.

Certainly.

I should be grieved to keep the lady waiting.

Count. (*Aside.*)

Plague on the woman! (*Aloud.*) There's no lady.

Countess.

What?

Count Philip, is this true?

Count.

How? is it true?

I've told you so; but if there were or no,

What would it matter?

Countess.

Matter? O my Philip!

Nay, I must tell you what is in my heart.

I love you, Philip; do not look so cold,—

I love you with the deep love of a woman;

This is no fleeting fancy of a girl

That hardly knows her mind, before it change.

O Philip, when the heart is young and soft,

It takes impressions easily as wax,

And each effaces other ;—but, alas,

When grown to womanhood, it takes the stamp

Of one loved form, and cannot crush it out,

But bears the impress with it to the grave.

And I *do* love you ; do not frown at me,

I cannot bear to see you frown at me ;

Nay, hear me, I am favourite of the Elector,

And I have but to ask, and he would give me

All wealth and honours, more than heart can

      wish ;

And these should be love offerings for my Philip.

And you should have promotion in the army,

And glory such as soldiers love ! but hear me,—

If you will none of these, then will I leave

My all but regal honours for your sake,

Wealth, houses, titles, all I fling away,

To follow you, my Philip, through the world.

COUNT

Pardon me, madam, this can never be ;

My heart is not my own, I cannot give
That which is not my own.

CinderELLA — no.

COUNTESS.

O Philip, Philip!
I did not think that I could fall so low :
O love, upon my knees I pray you love me,
Only so very little.   One kind look
Would cheer my heart, as some unlooked-for ray
Cheers a rain-beaten flower.

COUNT.

I pray you, rise,
Dear Countess, I do really pity you;
But more I cannot.   It were cruel kindness
To lull your heart to sleep with feignèd love;
Such sleep hath saddest waking.

COUNTESS.

Ay, it hath;
And I am now awake, for I have dreamed
A cursèd, foolish dream.   Pity me, Count!

Nay, keep your pity, it may be you'll need it

For other than for me.   What ! you have dared

To spurn my love, and trample on my heart,

And now you talk of pity ?   Know you then,

That those who deeply love, can *hate* as deeply,

And I have power, you dare not brave my hate !

But you are smiling, Philip ; ah, you know

I was but jesting when I spoke of hate.

You are too brave to tremble at my threats,

And so you'll try to love me, won't you, Philip ?

You'll give me back a little of my love.

O, do not shake your head ; what *have* I done

That you should goad me thus to madness, Philip ?

COUNT.

Nay, madam, pardon me—it cannot be :

I grieve to say it—but it cannot be—

'Tis my last word.

COUNTESS.

Be it so, Count Philip !

It may be that you fear not for yourself;

But there is one is dearer than yourself,

Leave me to find her out; and then, and then—

It shall go hard, but I will find the means

To drag her down to infamy—farewell. [*Exit.*

COUNT.

Most amiable Countess, fare you well—

Thank God she's gone! If women only knew

How men do loathe these favours thrust upon
   them,

They'd be less prodigal! To think that I

Could love a painted Jezebel like that!

A thing of paste and patches! Or that I

Could fling away that rosebud for this fungus!

Yet I half pitied the old doting fool,

To see her kneel, and whimper on my hand,

The while adown her rosy cheeks the tears

Had traced their channels. She, too, once so
   proud,

Who brow-beats the Electress in her palace !

O most sweet Countess ! Did she think her
       threats

Would drive me into love ? Nay, that indeed

Were taking hearts by storm—and yet, and yet

I tremble at her anger, lest it reach

The innocent head of my own, own Princess.

Spite of myself I dread that tongue of hers !

A woman's like a serpent ; for her tongue

Is her sole weapon, and it makes a wound

That leaves the venom in it.   O, should she

Find who her rival is, and whisper poison

Into the dull ear of the sottish Prince,

He might—O God, I cannot think of it !

So brutal is he in his drunken fury ;

Heaven grant me patience.   O, to think of her,

My priceless pearl, and given to such a swine !

My peerless lily, doomed to pine and die

'Mongst noisome docks and nettles ! O my God,

It shall not be ; but I will steal the pearl

And give it worthier setting ; and I'll plant

My flower in some fair garden, where the sun,

The great bright sun of love shall shine on her,

And she shall drink the honey'd dews of love.

I dare not dream such bliss, and yet it might be,

Had I but.half the courage of a man ! [*Exit.*

ACT II.

Scene I.

The Street, Gustav *and* Mary *meeting.*

Gustav.

WELL, this is lucky, you've saved me a walk; I was just going to see you.

Mary.

I'm sorry I can't return the compliment. But, pray why are you wrapped in a cloak, as if it were January?

Gustav.

Why, darling? Well, I thought it was going to rain;—indeed, I think it is now; besides, it's very chilly; don't you think so?

MARY.

No, I don't. That's all nonsense; you're not generally so much afraid of the weather,— look, sir, there's hardly a cloud to be seen. Gustav, you're hiding something, what is it?

GUSTAV.

Nay, dear, I swear—

MARY.

I *will* see (*opens his cloak and sees his arm bound up in surgical bandages*). Oh, Gustav, dearest, you're wounded (*cries*).

GUSTAV.

Don't cry, there's a dear; I only had a little accident this morning,—was thrown from my horse, that's all; but it's nothing, upon my honour.

MARY (*sobbing*).

I don't believe a word; you've been fighting again, you monster; about some girl too, I've no doubt; but you'll be killed some day, and then *I* won't cry for you.

GUSTAV.

Well, darling, if you'll only leave off crying *now*, and be reasonable, I'll tell you all about it. It was about a lady, certainly, but not one you need be jealous of; one of our fellows spoke rather too freely about the Princess, so I stopped his mouth by running him through the body; but the doctor says he'll get over it, as I've not touched a vital part. But, my dear girl, you must remember you are to be a soldier's wife, and you mustn't cry about such a scratch as this. Look here, dear, I've got something for you; here's a ring for your pretty little finger.

MARY.

O, Gustav dear, how can I thank you?

GUSTAV.

Ah, you know *how* well enough; that's my

own dear little Mary. But, stop, I've got something else, not for you though, this time. Here's a letter from the Count to the Princess.

MARY.

Poor thing! she'll be glad enough to get it; and yet I wish from my heart he wouldn't write to her. I've no patience with Philip; and if I thought it would do any good, I'd never lose an opportunity of saying the most ill-natured things of him to the Princess.

GUSTAV.

I wish you'd persuade her to run away with him, and then we'd all four of us go to England, or some other out-of-the-way place, and make the happiest little colony in the world.

MARY.

Well, I confess I don't think anybody could blame her much if she did. You don't know what she suffers at the hands of that wretched husband of hers; do you know, not long ago he struck her?

GUSTAV.

For God's sake, dear, don't tell me about it, you'll drive me wild. O, how I wish he were anything but the Crown Prince, that I might send my rapier through his heart (if he's got any), and then Philip should marry his widow.

MARY.

But, in the meanwhile, as he *is* the Crown Prince, and as that is out of the question, what *are* we to do? This love of theirs is sure to be found out soon, and then,—I dare not think of the consequence !

GUSTAV.

Well, dear, I've thought over the matter in all its bearings, and I can see but one of two ways out of the difficulty.—She *must* either give him up altogether, or run away with him;

him; I know you're going to tell me it's very wrong, and all that sort of thing, so it is, no doubt; but it's death to both of them to go on as they do now; and, moreover, it's a question I can't settle, whether carrying on this mockery of allegiance to a husband you detest is not as immoral as the other alternative.

MARY.

O, Gustav, you must not reason in this way, it's awfully wicked.

GUSTAV.

Ah, that's one of your English prejudices. Anyhow, dear, you'd better give her the letter at once; so I'll say good-bye!

MARY.

Good-bye,—I shall see you again soon?

GUSTAV.

Never fear, dearest.—*Au revoir.*   [*Exeunt.*

Scene II.

Count Königsmarkt's *house.   The* Count,
alone, singing, with his lute.

Song.

IF it is, as in love, or in sorrow,
    It seems, that thy tone
Is thy soul, O my lute, let it borrow
    Some notes from my own.

As the sun doth its hue to the sky give,
    The sky to the sea,
So my love, or its echo, will I give,
    My lute, unto thee.

Thy soul, till my fingers had skill'd it,
    Was silent, my lute;

And mine, till love touch'd it and thrill'd it,

      My own too was mute.

Now my soul hath a voice, let it cleave then

      To thine for relief;

Thou canst joy with its gladness, O grieve then,

      Awhile with its grief.

I cannot sing, my lute is out of tune,

Or else my heart is.—O my peerless queen!

I wonder has she got my letter yet?

Would I were there, my sighs should back my

      prayers,

My tears should melt her gentle heart to yielding;

But now she is alone, and the old thoughts,

The cold world's logic, like an icy stream,

Shall flood her heart and chill it; freeze again

What love had well-nigh thaw'd, as alpine snows,

That yield to the warm kisses of the sun,

Freeze up again at night.   How strange it seems

That thoughts like these can reach a heart like
    hers,
So poor a breath can blast so fair a flower.
Yet so it is ; though innocent herself,
She fears the judgment of an unjust world ;
She trembles lest the adder tongues of spite
Should hiss at her ; she fears those cursèd women
Who seem to think this damning vice in others
A virtue in itself, or dream that virtue
Is purchased at the cost of charity.
O, if the angels sing when sinners weep,
How do the devils joy when angels fall !
But this were not to fall, 'twere but to raise
Her body to her soul,—a resurrection
From that cold grave of love wherein she lies.
For she was mine, from earliest childhood mine ;
And though a thousand priests were paid to
    mumble
Their blessings on her cursèd union

They could not take her soul away from me,

To whom God gave it,—God is more than man,

The soul than is the body,—therefore I

Own more of her, and by a higher title,

Than he to whom man gave her.

          Enter GUSTAV.

                  Well, Gustav,

You gave my letter into Mary's hand ?

          GUSTAV.

Yes, Philip.

          COUNT.

          Thanks, for this and for the zeal

With which you back'd my cause ; but you'll

      forgive me

If I should think you almost over-zealous,

We cannot cut the throats of all the babblers ;

And failing this, your conduct, my Gustav,

Would rather fan suspicion than allay it.

We must be cautious.   It were just as well

That you spoke less with Mary in the street ;

I'm sure you'll pardon me, but people know

That you're my Damon, I another Pythias ;

They know, too, Mary's love for the Princess ;

Meet her at night, beneath the linden trees,

Or where you will, but in the open street

Meet her, Gustav, as mere acquaintance meet,

You understand, with bows of cool indifference,

And talk about the weather—what you will.

You'll tell her this, and she'll not be offended ;

She knows how many, and how precious lives

Hang on our prudence.

GUSTAV.

Philip, let me laugh ;

I should have look'd for wisdom from a fool,

Or candour from a courtier, just as soon

As prudence from your lips.   But, trust me,

Count,

I've come on purpose here to preach a sermon

From your own text; I only wish that you

Were half as cautious as I mean to be;

And as for Mary, she's the soul of prudence.

I'll pass her, if it please you, in the street,

And make amends in private. But for you,

This serenading cannot last much longer;

And I've been urging Mary all this morning,

And more than half persuaded her, to use

What influence she hath with the Princess

To cut this Gordian knot.

COUNT.

Thanks, dear Gustav,

I thank you both, and hope with all my heart

That she may have success where I have fail'd.

GUSTAV.

Well, I'm on duty at the palace, Philip,

And so must say good-bye.

COUNT.

Good-bye, Gustav.

[*Exeunt.*

SCENE III.

The Palace of Herrnhausen. The ELECTOR *and the* COUNTESS PLATEN *on one side of the door, and several* COURTIERS *on the other.*

ELECTOR.

WHAT news, my lovely Countess? what
is this
That brings you from Mount Plaisir
at this hour?
You, who were never known to rise till noon,
A very Cleopatra you for indolence,
Who, sipping coffee, chatting with your friends,
Or watching the mad circlings of the flies,
Or strip of living blue between the curtains,
Where leaves and tendrils sparkle in the sun,

Do cheat the day of half its wonted hours,

You here at Herrnhausen before noon!

With eyes all bloodshot, too, as though with
    weeping,

Or sleeplessness, or both! what is it, Countess?

COUNTESS.

Nothing, your Highness, I assure you, nothing,

But I was restless, and have hardly slept,

I really know not why, but being so

Am come to seek for consolation here

Upon the bosom of the man I love.

FIRST COURTIER.

Here's old Platen come all the way from
Mount Plaisir in the morning, to seek consolation
on the Elector's waistcoat.

SECOND COURTIER.

The dear little innocent, is she though?

THIRD COURTIER.

What's in the wind? Listen again.

ELECTOR.

That's kind, my Platen, and I thank you for it.

But, tell me, is there nothing I can do

To prove my thanks? Have you no nephew now

Who seeks commission in my guards? no cousin

Who craves some vacant living? Is it so?

I know how good you are to your relations;

And mine shall be the task, in serving them

To show my love for you.

FIRST COURTIER.

Confound them! they get all the good things.

I was looking out for the next vacant living

myself.

SECOND COURTIER.

You'd make a pretty parson, you would.

FIRST COURTIER.

Pray, why not I as well as another?

SECOND COURTIER.

Why, you believe in nothing, and I always

thought a modicum of faith was *de rigueur.*

FIRST COURTIER.

Not a bit of it,—on the contrary; that's just
what fits me for the post. My mind is an empty
vessel, into which you may pour any amount of
orthodoxy. There's no old wine there, to dis-
agree with the new, and burst the bottle; besides, do you suppose I wouldn't swallow faith,
like a bolus, if I could get any good by it?
Hush!

COUNTESS.

It is not that;
'Twas nothing but my love hath brought me here,
You know, my Prince, the love I bear to you;
I could not be your wife; nay, God is witness,
I would not you had stoop'd so low as I am;—
But I could follow you throughout the world,
Could watch your looks, forestall your lightest
wish,
And be your slave. And all for this, my Prince,

I've borne the slights and scornings of the world.

No words can tell what such as I endure;

But then the prize is greater than the pain,

When, having wept and waited all alone,

The sun at length shall dawn upon *our* night,

And shine on the poor flower that faints for him.

Ours are no duty kisses, like the wife's,

And cold as duty is.   She hath her pride,

Her name, and all the honours of her lord ;

We have our love, and that sufficeth us.

But O, if such as I may dare to say it,

Unworthy as we are, we make our own

His honour whom we love ;—ourselves have

    none ;

But, like a dog that dies without a murmur

To save the hand that strikes it, so are we.

They scorn us, and we heed it not ; nay rather,

As being proof of love, we welcome scorn ;—

But, should they lightly speak of him we love,

Or dare to taint the honour of his house,

They take our sun from heaven, and rob our

    souls

Of their one jewel; so that we shall die,

If we be weak; revenge, if we be strong.

ELECTOR.

Madam, I know your love; and from my heart

I thank you : but my honour, pardon me,

Is safe in my own keeping.

COUNTESS.

              O my Prince,

Think you I doubt your honour? That doth

    shine

Bright as the sun in heaven. But, as the sun

May be eclipsed by the speckled moon,

That draws her light and glory from the sun,

So may *her* shame, who owes whate'er she hath

Of fame to you, eclipse your princely honour.

O pardon me—'tis nothing but my love

That makes me bold.   Your love is as a rock

To which my heart is anchor'd; lost it that,

Then all indeed were lost;—yet this I risk,

Risk even your love, to save your honour,
     Prince;

And, now that I have dared to say so much,

I will not shirk my duty.   Hear me then :—

She, whom you honour'd more than all the
     world,

And gave her to your son to be his wife,

Forgetful of her duty, and his name,

Forgetful of the glory of your house,

Hath paid back shame for honour ;—Prince, I
     tell you,

Her paramour is Philip Königsmarkt.

ELECTOR.

Madam, I'll not believe it.   I have heard

The idle tongues that wag about a court

Have dared to link their names, but did not think

That such as you could stoop so low as this,

To be the slanderers' mouth-piece!—Shame on
  you!

My Königsmarkt, my paragon of guardsmen!

The very soul of honour!—And my child,

For I do love her as she were my child!

First Courtier.

Why, he's like Balaam, she wanted him to
curse her enemies, and lo! he doth nothing but
bless them.

Second Courtier.

Well, all I can say is, that if he's Balaam, the
Crown Prince is Balaam's ass.

Third Courtier.

That shows, my friend, your ignorance of the
Scriptures, for Balaam's ass was chiefly remark-
able for speaking, and no one can accuse a Crown
Prince of loquacity, who never opens his mouth
but to put something into it.   Listen again.

COUNTESS.

You wrong me, Prince, you wrong me, dearest
    lord !
What motive but my zeal could make me speak,
Zeal for my Prince's honour ? Think again ;
If you should take away my love from me,
Then should I die in silence.   You to me
Are as a god : and that which you have given
That may you take away.   But, when I see
    them
Bringing foul shame upon the man I love,
Hurting my Prince's honour, I *will* speak.
And, look you, this is no mere calumny,
I have the proofs—such damning proofs of
    wrong
As neither he nor she would dare to answer.
He comes beneath her balcony at night ;
Nay, climbs up to her window ; but to-day
He sent a letter to her, fixing, doubtless,

Some meeting for to-night. Do you, my Prince,

Place a few guards beneath her garden wall,

And you shall know if I have slander'd them,

And know that I have risk'd and said so much

Because the honour of your princely house

Is dearer to me even than my life.

Farewell, my noble Prince ; may God forgive

    you

For those harsh words that you have spoke to

    one

Who lives but for your love.

ELECTOR.

              Madam, farewell.

                 [*Exeunt.*

SCENE IV.

The Princess's Apartments. PRINCESS *and*
MARY.

PRINCESS.

 MARY, I am sad, and sick at heart;
Sing me, sweet Mary, for your voice,
like David's,
Can drive the fiend of sadness from my soul.

MARY.

What shall I sing?

PRINCESS.

Do you remember, dear?
The other day you sang a foolish song,
A silly love-song, and it ended with
Something about a harebell and a bee.

MARY.

Oh, I remember, this was it, I think.

SONG. (*He.*)

Come to my heart, my own,

Feel how it beats for you ;

Come, and I'll whisper alone, alone,

A something as sweet as true.

Come to my arms, my love,

See how they tremble—do ;

O, were I an angel above, above,

I'd barter heaven for you

Feel how my pulses beat,

Ask me not, darling, why ;

And, as for my secret sweet, my sweet,

You know it as well as I.

(*She.*)

There's a bee in a wild harebell,

Where honey and dew-drops glisten,

Hath he too a secret to tell, to tell

To her, that she seems to listen ?

He swings in the perfumed cup,

 And whispers his passionate vow;

But the honey he drinketh it up, all up,

 She knoweth his secret now.

(*He.*)

" O sweet is life," he saith,

 " And to drink of thy sweets at will;

But to die of thy honey'd breath, such death,

 My flower, were sweeter still."

(*She.*)

And the harebell doth but sigh;

 But he laughs, that roving bee,

" I will drink her poor heart dry, and fly

 To the lily that waits for me."

(*He.*)

" I shall die of grief," she thinks,

 " Of honey and love bereft;"

But the butterfly comes, and drinks, and drinks
What honey the bee hath left.

(*She.*)
And he hath splendid wings,
Of purple, and red, and gold,
And women are weak, poor things, poor things,
And the moral is trite and old.
[COUNT PHILIP *is heard singing*
in the garden.
But the bee hath flown, hath flown,
From the cup of the wild harebell,
He hath found the lily alone, alone,
The lily that loves him well.

And into her heart hath crept,
Till her white arms fold him over,
And the honey'd tear she hath wept, hath wept,
Is the welcome she gives her lover.

[*The* COUNT *enters.*

I would I were the bee, my own Princess,

To creep into that lily heart, and dwell there,

For ever and for ever.

PRINCESS.

O my Philip,

I knew that you would come again to-night,

Not from your letter only, but my heart;

I feel your coming ere I see your face,

Just as the sky at morning, ere the sun

Rise from his bed, doth feel his presence near,

And all that loving breast doth flush for joy.

But tell me, Philip, what are these new fears

Of which your letter speaks?

COUNT.

O, my own love,

God knows I would not fright you without

cause;—

But all our path of love is hedged with peril:

It is as 'twere a bridge of sweet flowers, thrown
Across a precipice. But listen, dearest ;—
The peril cometh on us, yet we stay ;
We see it coming, yet we flee not from it—
We flee it not, though flight were life indeed,
And this is death indeed—the soul's death first,
And then the body's.

PRINCESS.

Be content, my Philip,
You have my soul, what signifies the rest ?

[MARY, *who had gone out, re-enters
in haste.*

MARY.

Count Philip, you are watch'd. Two men are station'd,
Arm'd to the teeth, before the garden gate.

PRINCESS.

Fly, fly, my Philip !

COUNT.

Do not fear for me—
They shall not see me—I will climb the wall,
And leap the ditch, and make across the fields.
This is some plot of that old Countess Platen.
Beware her, dearest.

PRINCESS.

O, I will, I will,
But fly, or they will take you.

COUNT.

Sweetest love,
Think, if you would, I need not fly you thus,
But day and night be near you.

PRINCESS.

Leave me now,
And save your life, my Philip, for my sake—
It is the dearest boon that you can give me—
Good night, good night.

COUNT.

Until to-morrow, love,
Good night. O say it once, a moment, thus—
Your heart to mine—Good night.

[*He descends from the balcony, and exit.*

PRINCESS.

.   Save him, my God!
See, he hath reach'd the ground, and cross'd the
        lawn,
And now hath climb'd the wall. He waves his
        hand—
" Good night!" Now he is gone. Pray for him,
        Mary ;
For you are pure, and need not fear to pray,
And maybe God will bless him for your prayers.

Scene V.

The Elector's Palace at Herrnhausen. The Elector *and* Philip Königsmarkt.

Elector.

COUNT PHILIP, I am glad that you
are here,
For I have much to tell you.   There
is one
Hath crept into my heart, and nestled there,
A little robin in a wither'd tree;
And if you steal my robin I shall die,
For I am old, and have not long to live;
And if it be that I have dream'd a dream,
So sweet a dream it was, I fain would die,
If that might be, unwaken'd.   Hear me, then,
I speak not as a monarch to his subject,
But as an old man, pleading for his child—

The child of his old age.—Say she is innocent,

'Twould break my heart to think her aught but

pure.

COUNT.

Prince, she is innocent, as God is just.

ELECTOR.

I knew it; thank you, Count. Give me your hand,

It is a brave man's hand, the hand of one

Who would not wish to break an old man's heart,

And drag her down to ruin whom he loves.

But you must go, for her sake, you must go,

To save her name from base and sland'rous

tongues,

That spit their venom at her; for the sun

May be obscured and darken'd by the smoke

Of noisome weeds; and this infernal slander

Would blight an angel's fame, and stain the robe

Of innocence herself, and by your presence

You give the slanderer a weapon, Count,

To wound her name withal.   You'll leave to-night

See, I have here a letter for the Prince,

Frederic Augustus, of the imperial army,

Herein I do intreat the Prince to place you

Upon his staff, and give you full occasion

To gain the glory that you love so much;

And so my darling shall be saved, and you

Shall win your spurs.   You'll start at once.

                    COUNT.

                              My Prince,

You'll give me till to-morrow?

                    ELECTOR.

                              No, to-night;

You must not see her, Count, before you go.

                    COUNT.

It shall be so, your Highness.   Fare you well

                              [*Exit.*

(*An interval of a few months is supposed to take*

   place between the second and third acts, during

   which the campaign is concluded.)

ACT III.

Scene I.

A room in-the Countess Platen's house of Mount Plaisir. COUNTESS alone, Servant brings in a letter.

SERVANT.

MADAM, a servant of Count Königsmarkt
Hath brought this letter, and will
wait an answer.

COUNTESS.

Tell him to wait.   And look you, see you give
him
The best of meat and drink—whate'er he asks:
Now you may leave me.   [*Exit* Servant.

What! the Count come back,
And warning me the first of his arrival!
I see it now, my prodigal return'd
Hastens to ask forgiveness. Thank you, Philip,
You will not find me cruel; yet indeed
I might have guess'd as much; I might have
        known
The seed of love sown in such fruitful soil
Would bear some fruit at last.—O I have sown
In bitter tears, to reap in fuller joy.
O Philip, my own Philip, how I love thee!
This note shall be the first link in the chain,
The strong love-chain, to bind us heart to heart.
Yet it were well perhaps to frown at first,
To seem a little cruel, lest he deem
His conquest all too easy; till at length
My love shall burst all barriers, like a torrent,
And I will bid him take his fill of love.
Philip, I kiss the note your hand hath press'd;

How my hand trembles as I open it!

Poor foolish hand, and foolish, fluttering heart,

Be still, and let me read.—Why, what's this?—

    " Madam?"—

That would seem cold were it not diffidence—

" You have a certain ribbon, that was bound

About the colours of my regiment"—

Well, if I have, why does he plague me now

About a foolish ribbon?—" This is mine;

It was the prize of some athletic games;

And given me by the Princess.   Pray you,

    madam,

Return it by the bearer of this letter,

And all shall be forgiven."   Death and fury!

He dares to mock me thus! this cursed ribbon—

And given him by the Princess.   O, my God!

Am I to be their go-between? is he

To trample on my heart to reach to hers?

" And all shall be forgiven," generous Count!

As though not he, but *I*, had done the wrong.

But patience, patience, do not break, my heart;

And I will give thee vengeance for thy love.

Let me read on.   What's this?—" forgiven"—

     well?—

" If not, and you refuse to give it up,

Look to yourself, for I have sworn to have it.

Yours, as you answer, Philip Königsmarkt."

A challenge to a woman! gallant Count;

Poor fool! I have thee now.   With this blue

     ribbon

I'll bait a hook to catch thy life withal!

O God, to think that I could once have stoop'd

To ask this shallow trifler for his love!

It drives me mad to think it.—Thank you, Philip,

You saved me from myself; why, this same love

Levels all intellects; and makes a woman

Hang on the vapid mouthings of her lord,

With bated breath, as on an oracle.

But that's all over now, and I'm awaken'd

From a brief, foolish dream.—Revenge, revenge,

It is the nobler passion.   Let me think—

This woman's brain of mine is all confused—

I must be careful not to rouse suspicion ;

But lull his heart to sleep with promises.

How shall I write ? will this do ?—" Dear Count

   Philip,

I thank you for your letter, though its tone

Was hardly kind or courteous ; for indeed

I know not how I have offended you,

My only fault was loving you too well.

To this I must plead guilty, and the shame

To have my love rejected ; but for this

I think that you should rather pity me,

Than crush me with your anger.—For the ribbon,

I know not quite where I have laid it, Philip ;

But when I find it, I will send it you ;

And, though it grieve me that you value so

A present from another than from me,

I will bear this, and more than this, from you."

How shall I sign myself? Ah, this will do—

" Yours ever, spite of all your cruelty,

The Countess Platen."   Now then, Königs-

    markt,

Look to your arms, for you and I are match'd,

And you'll have need of them.   [*Rings.*

        Enter SERVANT.

            You'll give this letter

To the Count's servant.   [*Exit* Servant.

          Now, then, for my plans.—

'Tis well that I obtain'd from the Elector

That order for Count Königsmarkt's arrest;

If ever he revisit the Princess

I have him in my clutches—then, indeed,

It shall go hard but I will mar their joy.

But first to see the guards; 'tis well again

I took those two Italians in my pay—

They'll silence him, and I will silence them.

But what if he be grown more circumspect,

And come not as of old, or at a time

When least expected? I must lure him

    then;—

If I could only ask him in her name—

But he'd detect the forgery; and I

Should be a laughing-stock for both—What's

    that?

        [MARY *heard singing in the Street.*

        SONG.

There's a sound in the summer trees,

   That the dew-drops christen,

There's a voice in the summer trees—

    Listen, listen.

Through the moonlit haze they glisten,

   Like the islands in fairy seas;

But, O, there's a sound that's more than these—

    Listen, listen.

'Tis the voice of my own, my own,
 Calling, calling ;
And I must to him alone, alone,
 While the dews are falling, falling,
 While the dews are falling.

COUNTESS.

Why, that's Miss Dillon—Mary, as they call
 her,—
Of all the world, the person suited best
To be my instrument. I'll call her in. [*Calls.*
Good day, sweet Mistress Mary ; may I beg
You'll turn aside, and spend an hour with me.
I've news to tell, that you were loth to lose—
News of the army—where a friend of yours
Doth battle like a Paladin of old.

MARY.

Good morrow, Madam. (*Aside.*) How ! she calls
 me " Mary,"
Invites me to her house ! What can it mean ?

The more she smiles, the more I tremble at her;—

And yet, if she had news of poor Gustav—

If he were sick or wounded, and she told me

That I might go and nurse him—then I think

That I could almost bless her for her news.

I hardly like to enter, for I know

She's the Princess' enemy, and yet

It's long since I have heard from poor Gustav;

I *must* go in, although my mind misgives me.

[Enters the room.

Madam, I wait your pleasure, thanking you

For that you seem to take an interest

In one so humble.

COUNTESS.

Mary, prithee come

Into this inner room, where we may speak,

And fear no interruption.

[They enter the inner room.

As I hear,

You have a lover in the Prince's army—
One named Gustav.

MARY.

Yes, Madam, it is true ;
And you have news of him ?—He is not ill
Or wounded ?

COUNTESS.

Neither sick nor wounded, Mary.

MARY.

Thank God for that.

COUNTESS.

Nay, keep your gratitude,
Until you know the worst.

MARY.

The worst ! O, Madam,
For God's sake, speak.

COUNTESS.

Well, Mary, it appears
This cavalier of yours is somewhat choleric—

It is a common failing in the army—
And mind, if ever he escape from this,
I warn you of his temper.

MARY.

Heavens! Madam,
You mean to drive me mad.

COUNTESS.

Nay, patience, patience;
I'll to my story.   Well, it seems, Gustav,
Meeting a friend, hot-headed as himself,
Invited him to share a flask of wine,
And then another, maybe even a third.
These they discussed in perfect harmony;
But, being somewhat heated with their wine,
They got to bandying words about some trifle,
Compared, perhaps, the colour of your eyes
With those of his friend's mistress—anyhow,
From words they came to blows; from blows to
    sword-thrusts ;—

Gustav was scarcely scratch'd, but his poor friend

Was wounded in the lungs, and died, alas !

Without the power of utterance.

MARY.

O my God !

COUNTESS.

Yet is the worst to tell : for, as this duel

Was without witnesses, the dead man's friends

Accused Gustav of murder : as, moreover,

All duels are forbidden in the army,

He is condemn'd—I grieve to say—to death.

[MARY *falls forward on her face,*
and faints.

Poor lovesick fool ! I almost pity her !

And yet she's happier in this love of hers,

Than I with my revenge.—But I must rouse her,

Or she will lose what little wits she hath.

[*Throws water over her.* MARY
comes to herself.

MARY.

I thank you, Madam; I am better now,

Only a little weak; but speak, I pray you—

I think that I could almost bear it now.

Where is he, Madam? I must go to him,

And see the Prince, and kneel before the
judges—

Who knows what precious moments I am
wasting?

COUNTESS.

Poor Mary, you are very weak and ill—

Drink this—'twill give you strength.

        [*Gives wine, which* MARY *drinks.*

        Now will I tell you:—

You cannot see the Prince, nor move the
judges;—

'Twere worse than useless, it were losing time;

Yet is there time and hope.—'Twas but this
morning

Count Philip Königsmarkt return'd to Hanover,

And wrote me this sad story. Said, moreover,

That as Gustav had served with honour once

Here, in the Elector's guards, if he (the

    Elector)

Would speak a good word for him to the Prince,

Pledging his princely word that he was brave,

And all incapable of such a deed,

That then the Prince would doubtless spare his

    life.

Now, Mary, there is one, and only one

Can make him say the word. Put trust in me ;

I'll make him speak, and save your lover's life.

MARY.

O Madam, God will bless you, as do I :

Here, on my knees, I dedicate my life

To prove my thanks. Command me as you

    will—

I am your slave.

COUNTESS.

Thanks, thanks, my gentle slave ;

You'll find my service light.   And herewithal,

To test your gratitude, I order you

To write a letter for me to Count Philip.

MARY.

Dear Madam, would it were a harder task ;

But, hard or light, I hasten to obey.

[*Takes pen and paper.*

I wait for your dictation.

[COUNTESS *dictates, and* MARY *writes.*

" Dear Count Philip,

My mistress, having heard of your return,

Wishes to see you."—

MARY.

Yes, from this day forth

You *are* my mistress, Madam.

COUNTESS *continues.*

" She herself

Has burnt her hand, or she would write to you :

You know the little door that leads direct

To her apartments ; you'll be there to-night.

    " Yours, MARY DILLON."

        [COUNTESS *takes the letter.*

    MARY.

        Nay, but, dearest Madam,

If you should send the letter, worded thus,

He might, you'll pardon me—nay, he *would* think

    think

It came from the Princess.

    COUNTESS.

        What matter, Mary ?

After long absence it were common kindness

To reunite such loving hearts as those.

    MARY (*starting up*).

I am betrayed !   O God, I see it now !

Madam, it was a cruel, wicked lie !

Give me the letter.—

COUNTESS.

What? and poor Gustav!
I really pity him, to die so young,
And by a felon's death! And all because
His pretty Mary, whom he loved so well,
Refused to save his life.

MARY.

O Madam, Madam,
You cannot be so cruel as you seem—
You'll give me back my letter and my love,
My poor, poor love, so young, so very young!
I know you'll speak the word will save his
    life.—
I think I'm very ill, perhaps I'm dying.
Before I die, I'll kneel to you, sweet lady—
Pray you have mercy, as you hope for mercy,
As all have need of it. O mercy, mercy,
I think I'm dying now.

[*Falls forward.*

COUNTESS.

Not yet, sweet Mary—

Girls do not die of love so easily;

But, if you wake before to-morrow morn,

My druggist has deceived me. So, good night!

I'll lock you in, and wish you pleasant dreams.

Now for my task. I'll send the letter straight,

And then—and then—I think, my gay Count
         Philip,

I have you in a trap—and you shall find

That women too have weapons, and can use
         them.   [*Exit.*

SCENE II.

The Princess' Apartments. PRINCESS *and*
Attendants.

PRINCESS.

AS any one seen Mary since this
morning?

ATTENDANTS.

Not I, nor I, nor I.

MAID OF HONOUR.

May it please your highness,
I met her some time between nine and ten,
Pass down toward Mount Plaisir; and I think
She must have paid a visit to the Countess,
For when I turn'd soon after, she was gone;
Yet, had she kept the road, I must have seen
her.

PRINCESS.

This is strange news indeed.   Will some of you

Run to the Countess Platen's, and inquire

If Mary has been there, and when she left,

And where she went to after.   See, in short,

You come not back without some news of her.

Nay, all of you, go each a different way,

I cannot rest in this uncertainty.

                [*Exeunt* Maids of Honour.

Alone, alone—I long'd that they should leave

     me;

Yet now I cannot bear to be alone ;

Oh, what a weariness is this my life !

It seems to wander on, as some dull stream,

That cannot rest, nor sparkle in the sun,

Nor dally with the wild-flowers on its banks,

Creeps slowly on to what ?—to death ? Aye,

     death

That only makes life possible.   Without it

Man could not live, as without hope of rest

He could not labour.   Yet, if this be true,

Why do the market-girls that pass the gate,

Trudge singing to their work? What is their life?

'Tis hardly thought of death that makes *them*

     sing;

Yet, is it sweet to toil from morn to night,

To eat a scanty crust beneath a hedge,

To hear the children cry aloud for food?

Or is it that their life, with all its sorrows,

Hath the one joy denied to such as I am,

The one Eve's apple of our Paradise?

What is't to be a Princess? 'Tis to lie

On silken beds, whereon I cannot sleep;

Be served with dainty food I cannot eat,

And be denied the thing my soul delights in.

                        [*Walks to the window.*

There is a halo round the moon to-night,

It is a waning moon; and, as it walks

Alone, before a crowd of throbbing stars,

It minds me of some saint, who walks to death

Before a gaping multitude.   I wonder

If there are queens dwelling in yonder stars

Who may not love ; if there are hearts to sell,

And crowns to buy them with ; if there, as here,

Are peasant girls that sing, and queens that weep,

And fools that envy them.   'Tis like enough.

O, I am very sad, and sick at heart !

It seems so lonely without Mary here

To sing to me, and prattle of her love ;—

But where is she ? There is some mystery

In this strange visit to the Countess Platen ;

She cannot have betray'd me, yet I know not :

She is a woman, and I've trusted her.—

'Tis very long since I have heard of Philip,—

Here's his last letter.—If I could, I'd chide him

For that he writes too lovingly ;—and yet,

God knows I would not have it otherwise.

I wonder where he is, and what he's doing;—
If I could make myself invisible,
I'd fly to him, and kiss him as he sleeps,
And make him dream of me.

[PHILIP, *who has entered unperceived.*

No need of that,
My own, own love—my first and only love.

PRINCESS.

Philip !

COUNT.

Why, love, you seem amazed to see me,
As though I were not looked for.

PRINCESS.

Philip ! Philip !

COUNT.

Nay, dearest, speak to me, but not so wildly,
You wrote me word to come, and I am here.

PRINCESS.

I wrote you word to come ?

CsOUNT.

Not you yourself,

But you bade Mary write.—Look, here's her

letter,

This is her writing. " She herself," that's you,

" Has burnt her hand, or she would write to

you.

You know the little door that leads direct

To her apartments ; you'll be there to-night."

See, there's the letter, love, and here am I.

And yet you feign surprise.   Show me the

wound,

That I may kiss it well.

PRINCESS.

O God ! my Philip,

This is some wicked plot ; it was not I

That bade her write.   I knew not you were

here.

O, fly at once, ere yet it be too late !

Fly, for my sake, dear Philip.　Kiss me once—
One long, long kiss—I somehow fancy, dear,
'Twill not be *quite* the last.

COUNT.

My own, own queen,
I must obey, though tempted to rebel.
Fear not for me ; but write to-morrow morn,
When we may meet again.

PRINCESS.

I will.—Good night.

[*Exit* COUNT.

God, and His angels, keep him from all harm.

Scene III.

*The Staircase below the Princess' Apartments.—
Guards stationed there; among them the two
Italians in* Countess Platen's *pay.*

First Italian (*aside to the other*).

YOU know what we've got to do.

Second Italian.

Yes, I know well enough, and I
confess I don't like it.   An elopement, now, is
more to my taste; but these confounded German
women run away of themselves, so I'm afraid
we shan't do much business in that line.

First Italian.

Well, I should be ashamed of myself, if I were
such a white-livered hound as you.   Why, if it
weren't for a little affair of this kind now and

then, we should starve, or have to turn honest men, in sheer desperation.

SECOND ITALIAN.

Well, I'm not brave, I own. All men have their virtues; cunning's mine. But—quiet and keep back, here he comes.   [*Enter* PHILIP.

FIRST GUARD.

Count Königsmarkt, you can't pass.

COUNT.

Make way, fellow! You stop me at your peril.

GUARDS.

We'll see to that; you don't pass.

[COUNT *draws his sword.*

COUNT.

Ha! I'm ashamed to draw on such vermin. Out of my way! I prefer not treading upon worms. (*The Guards draw, and fall on him.*) What! only six scoundrels to one honest man?

That's not fair—they should have set a dozen such hounds as you on. There, I'm sorry to cheat the hangman, and dirty my sword. But it's a good deed, ridding the world of such ugly rascals. There goes one, and there's another, now here goes for a third. (*Three fall; but one of the Italians throws a cloak over his head, and he is run through, and falls.*) Well, I had hoped to die at a brave man's hand. It's rather hard to be killed by such a pitiful scoundrel. But if you've any humanity left in you, carry me from here. (*Aside.*) I wouldn't that my poor darling saw me here for a thousand lives.

Enter the COUNTESS PLATEN.

COUNTESS.

What! is it come to this, Count Königsmarkt? You cannot shun me now, nor scorn me now. But times are alter'd since I knelt to you,

And offer'd you my love, and you refused it.

You thought 'twas safe to trample on my heart;

But 'twas as one should think to crush a worm,

And tread upon an adder: 'twas a blunder.

So that poor writhing creature at my feet

Was once the proud Count Philip.

COUNT.

Gentle lady,

I fain would die in peace, for I have been

A most unwilling target for your shafts

Of love and hate by turns. This hate is cruel,

But O, the love was harder far to bear.

But pray you leave me—I am dying now,

And have not strength to bandy words with you.

COUNTESS.

Will you stand by, and hear him mock me thus?

An you were men, you'd stop his cursèd mouth.

FIRST GUARD.

Had we been men we had not done this deed;

And were you less a fiend, and more a woman,
You had not bribed us to it.   Take your
   money—
Would God that I could cast my crime from me
As I fling this away.   [*Throws down the money.*

CnowTESS.

                What, traitors ! dogs !
This language, and to me !

GUARD.

                Be silent, woman !
For very shame be silent.

COUNT.

                O, my own,
I would have seen you once before I died ;—
But maybe it is better as it is—
It's growing dark and cold.   Good night, good
   night.   [*Dies.*

Enter PRINCESS.
O, love, I have been dreaming—such a dream !

I thought that you were fighting, and were
    wounded;
And then I heard the clash of many swords:
But O, thank God, 'twas nothing but a dream.
But you're asleep, too, Philip.   Philip dear!
How sound he sleeps ; he must be very weary.
Is he not beautiful? My gentle Philip!
But, when he wakes, you'll see his great blue
    eyes,
So blue and deep, they almost frighten me.
Do you know, sometimes, in looking into them,
I seem to gaze into a deep blue lake,
Down, down, and down.   Hush! do not wake
    him up;
Pray you, watch by him, while I gather flowers.
Not you—you are a woman;—you, sir, please,
You are a soldier—I'll be back ere long.
What flowers will he love best? When we were
    children,

I used to fetch him early violets;

So now I'll make a violet wreath, and twine it

In his brown hair without awaking him,

And when he wakes we'll laugh at him.   But

      stop!

I fear me much, the violets are all dead—

Dead! dead! Which of you spoke of being dead?

Philip dear, wake! you frighten me—Dead!

     dead!   [*She falls fainting on his body.*

Enter GUSTAV *hastily, with a doctor.*

GUSTAV.

Too late! too late! And yet I pray'd and

    pray'd

That we might be in time to save him. See,

His nervous arm is weaker than a woman's,

And his poor hand, so often clasped in mine,

Cannot return my pressure. Sooth, good Doctor,

Your offices are useless.   Yet, my God!

Had I but known a few short moments sooner,

I might have saved him. But it's too late now.

I cannot help my tears ; and you would weep,

Had you but known him half so well as I did.

He was so brave, so full of gentleness !

Why, the worst hurt he ever got in battle

Was given him by a wounded enemy,

Whom he had tried to save. Ah ! who are these ?

Are these the cursèd miscreants who have killed

     him ?   [*Rushes at Guards, who escape.*

Too late again ! But all goes wrong to-day :

But I was blinded with these woman's tears—

See, I have broke my sword against the wall :

It might have served me for a pass like this :

But all goes wrong, all wrong. Why, 'twas my

     Mary,

My own, own Mary, by her meddling folly,

That brought this sorrow on us. It would seem

A woman must be either knave or fool.

Did she not know this wicked Jezebel,

That she must be her tool?—O, Countess,

   Countess,

This was indeed a villany to boast of!

I know I flatter you—to such as you are

'Tis something, this pre-eminence in vice;

Madam, I wish you joy of this your triumph.

Out of my sight! I would not harm the devil,

Took he a woman's guise.

     Countess.

      Most gallant warrior,

You need not waste your valour on a woman—

I leave you to your tears.   [*Exit.*

     Gustav.

      Thank God she's gone!

Good Doctor, will you see to the Princess?

Poor thing! I'd rather she should sleep for ever,

Than wake to such as this. [*Enter* Mary.

      O Mary, Mary,

'Twere better you had died, than lived to quench
That valiant soul, and break this loving heart!
Aye, weep your eyes out, child! 'Tis well to
    weep;
'Tis all is left us now.

             MARY.

               God knows, Gustav,
I am not here to justify myself;
I will not ask you, dear, to love me more.
I'm come to say good-bye, and then to leave you.
Good-bye.

             GUSTAV.

     Good-bye.

         Will you not kiss me once?

       [*He kisses her.* *Exit* MARY.

             GUSTAV.

She came to say good-bye, and then to leave me.
What did she mean? Where is she gone to?

     Mary!

God! should she do herself an injury!

Why, I was mad to let her leave me thus.

Mary, my own!—no answer; Mary, Mary!

[*Exit, calling her.*

Re-enters with MARY.

Forgive me, my own love, for I have wrong'd
    you;

But I was mad, and knew not what I said.

I cannot blame you, dear, that you were made

The tool of that vile woman. She'd have found

A hundred other ways to kill poor Philip,

Had this one failed.   But you were ever guile-
    less,

Knowing no wrong, and thinking none in others.

Forgive me, Mary.

MARY.

O Gustav, Gustav,

I too should ask forgiveness.   Yet I cannot,

For in myself I find no room for pardon.

Yet 'twas my love for you that made me weak.

Oh, when I woke up from my opiate sleep,

And saw you bending over me, I thought,

I thought that that was heaven, and you,
    Gustav,

Were some kind angel sent to comfort me.

GUSTAV.

Thank God, my own, I found you when I did;

But dry your eyes, dear Mary, dry your eyes—

You will have need of all your strength to-night.

See to the poor Princess, and try to soothe her;

I fear me she's beyond all reach of comfort—

May God deal gently with her in her sorrow;

I leave her to your care—good night.

MARY.

Good night.

SCENE IV.

A Family Council assembled, consisting of the ELECTOR, *the* CROWN PRINCE, *and others. Before them the* PRINCESS, *brought up for trial.*

ELECTOR.

OPHIA DOROTHEA, you are sum-
mon'd
To speak, as you will answer to your
God,
To certain charges that are brought against you.
You stand accused of having entertained
The late Count Philip Königsmarkt, at night,
In your apartments; and, at various times,
Of having corresponded with the Count,
When he was absent with the Imperial Army.
I cannot make a speech to you, my child;
It breaks my heart to see you standing there—

But I am sure that you are innocent :

And yet this interview of yesternight,

And its sad end, have raised a scandal here

That must be laid to rest, so that our house

May bear no stain upon its proud escutcheon.

PRINCESS.

I pray you, father, who are mine accusers?

COUNTESS.

So please your Highness, I, the Countess Platen.

PRINCESS.

My father, I am fallen very low,

But not so low that I can deign to speak

To such as she is.   Were it otherwise,

I could show proof the letter came from her

That lured Count Philip to this interview ;

That it was she who placed upon the stairs

That ambuscade of soldiers, in her pay,

With orders for his murder.—See, she trembles!

But I am here to speak of other matters

Than of her crimes.   What would you learn of
  me?
Whether I loved Count Philip Königsmarkt?
Ay, from my soul I loved him, O my father.
Why, from our earliest childhood he to me
Was as a little God—so much more noble
And beautiful he seem'd than all the rest.
And, when my gentle Philip grew to manhood,
And left my father's court to be a soldier,
I check'd my tears to tell his gallant deeds.
Loved him ! Why, if they only breathed his
  name,
I felt the blood rush madly through my veins,
And riot at my heart.   If this was love,
Why then I loved poor Philip.   For the rest,
You know the rest; and how they married me:
It was a golden chain with which they bound
  me ;
It could not bind my soul, for that was Philip's.

Ay, I did love him ; and from time to time

We met, and told each other of our love.

Of this much I am guilty, but no more :

For I was faithful to the cruel vow

That others laid upon me.—And, for proof,

I pray you, father, summon here a priest,

And bid him bring the holy elements.

ELECTOR.

It shall be as you wish.—Will one of you

Go hence and bring a minister of God ?

[*Exit* Attendant, *who returns with*

Minister.

PRINCESS.

I thank you.—Pray you consecrate the cup.

This is the cup of God ; and by His blood

I call my God to witness to my truth.

[*Drinks.*

Now, will you give the cup to mine accuser,

And bid her drink ? Why does she hesitate ?

She need not fear, for she is innocent.

She dare not drink of it! Is then the accused

Less guilty than the accuser?

[COUNTESS *refuses the cup.*

CROWN PRINCE.

Hold! Enough!

Who cares to know these different shades of

    guilt?

Guilty or not, I've done with her.

ELECTOR.

My child,

I do believe you innocent;—and yet,

After this full confession you have made,

I cannot hold you blameless. You have err'd

Through too much loving; and to such as you

Shall doubtless much be pardon'd. But mean-

    while

You cannot live with one you cannot love.

You must not stay in Hanover, to be

The talk of idle courtiers, and the target
For poison'd shafts of irony, the toast
Of drunken soldiers' revels. You must go
To where, in sorrow and in solitude,
You may repent you of your fault, and ask
For mercy at the throne of mercy. Therefore,
If it be pleasing to the Prince, your husband—

CROWN PRINCE.

Do with her as you will—

ELECTOR.

My sentence is,
That you be banish'd unto Ahlden Castle
During our pleasure. Like you this, my son?

CROWN PRINCE.

Ay, vastly well. And if she stay at Ahlden
Until I ask her back, she's like, methinks,
To tarry long enough.

ELECTOR.

Farewell, my child :

It breaks my heart to say the word farewell.

Come here, and let me hold you to my heart,

Only a moment—now good bye, good bye.

God's blessing go with you.

PRINCESS.

Farewell, my father,

And you, my lord, farewell.

[*Exeunt* ELECTOR, CROWN PRINCE,

and others.

All over now;

All over.—Philip, gentle Philip, my own love,

Can he be dead? Why, only yesternight

He spoke to me in his old low, sweet voice,

And shall I never hear his voice again?

His voice, that seem'd familiar as my own?

Nor look into his great blue speaking eyes?

It cannot be! it must be but a dream,

And I shall wake, and see my love again,

As when he sang his last sweet song to me:

" But the bee hath flown, hath flown
 From the cup of the wild harebell;
He hath found the lily alone, alone,
 The lily that loves him well."

He was the bee, and I that loved him well,
I was the lily; yet they ask'd but now
If that I loved him! Loved him? Loved my
 Philip?
I could have laugh'd.—But stop! I'm going
 mad!
Mad! why not mad? why, what hath madness
 in it
That I should dread it? Is it to be mad,
To see my Philip near me day and night,
To hear his soft voice whisper as of old?
And is it reason, dreaming he is dead?
Let me go mad, or die.—O Philip, Philip,
Come to me, love, and take me far away

To some lone isle in undiscover'd seas,

Where we may wander under myrtle groves,

And hear the song-birds' rapture all night long.

Come to me, love—I wait for thee—come,

come !

SONNET.

ON THE BEACH, NEAR LYME REGIS.

HE mist is on the sea, and clinging fast
   To blindly peering headlands, but
     the waves
Come surging from the shroud, as from their
   graves
Come angry figures of the dreamy past ;
When all the house is hush'd, and sleep at last
Has left us.—On they come, with anger pale,
   And fling them down, and die, with sudden
     shocks
   Of impotent rage ; while from the sullen rocks
Come mocking echoes of a dying wail.—

I stand between the echoes and the strife,

    As between life and death, a life that seems

    A weary, wavelike rush of aimless schemes ;

And death a grinning mockery of a life ;

A waking without sight, a sleep without its

    dreams !

SONNET.

AFTER STORM IN SUMMER.

HE young leaves lie in heaps upon the
    ground,
    Like Herod's murder'd innocents.—
Last night
From the dark forest came a wailing sound
  Of mother trees, that toss'd in piteous plight
Their ravished arms.—To-day the storm hath
    sped,
  Like the death angel, over lands and seas,
  Marking his track with ruin.   What are these
Poor leaves, that we should note them being dead?
So tears the life-storm from our hearts their first

And fairest ; Love, that into our young souls

Breathed the warm breath of life ; and Faith,
that rolls

Back the cloud-gates of Heaven ; then Hope,
that erst

Planted sweet flowers by each memorial stone ;

Till, like a forest stript, our hearts are left alone.

SONNET.

THE child unquestioning treads his
    father's path ;
    Then he becomes a man ; and lifts
  his eyes,
And lo, a thousand guiding beacons rise,
Pointing all ways to Heaven ; and, in his wrath,
Saith, " I will none of these, far better none
  Than false guides leading me I know not
  where.
  Silence is meeter than unmeaning prayer."
And so the poor soul staggers blindly on.
Then he grows old ; and feels within a sad,
  Sad void, and sees perhaps the light

Of Faith in dying eyes ; or hears at night
The solemn Christmas bells. Then is he glad,
And seeks again the path his childhood trod.
For divers are the roads, yet all may lead to God.

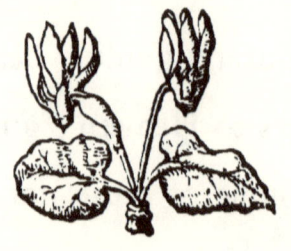

SONNET.

THEY rise above the forest, like a
dream ;
Silent, from wooded base to granite
crest ;
So silent, and so beautiful, they seem
As earth had of her choicest and her best
Built her God's altar. There the white clouds
rest,
Lovingly clinging ; as fair children cling
About some stern old warrior, till he smile ;
Or as white pigeons on unwearied wing
Circle around some grey cathedral pile,

I

Nestling in storied niche of saint or king.

Here in the woods a thousand streamlets sing,

    Bringing glad tidings to the thirsty earth ;

Ere to far seas they wander murmuring,

    Like silver chains of life, uniting death and

        birth.

THE moon had risen in haste, and left her zone
Of silver, set with diamonds, on the breast
Of her great lord, the sea, who, left alone,
Heaved in his sleep, and murmur'd for unrest.
His white hands, feeling feebly o'er the sand,
Clasp'd the tall cliffs, fondling their rugged feet,
While his true heart's tumultuous pulses beat ;
For still he dream'd his love was nigh at hand :
Dream on, poor heart, for morn will soon be breaking,
And thou shalt know that thou art left alone,
Know that our sorrows come too oft at waking,
That but in dreams are love and joy our own.

FAREWELL.

ONCE again, my own, my Margaret,
  Let me see thee as thou art:
  Let us talk while time is left us,
Soul with soul, and heart with heart.

Let me see thee in thy beauty,
  O my Margaret, as of old;
Let thy tresses fall around thee
  In a cataract of gold.

Let me drink thy dewy kisses,
  Let me breathe thy perfumed sighs;
Let me see mine image floating
  In the glory of thine eyes.

Few and short the hours before us,
  Let us use them while we may :
Time enough for weeping, dearest,
  When thy darling is away.

If it must be, love must perish,
  Hopes be shatter'd one by one,
Let our love, that seem'd eternal,
  Die in splendour, like the sun.

Soon will he be rising, Margaret,
  Like a giant in his might,
Flinging off the chains of darkness
  That have bound him through the night.

Ere the dew-drops leave the meadows,
  And the daisies ope their eyes,
I must go, and leave for others
  All my heart had learn'd to prize.

Blind our passion, deep our sorrow,
   We have sown, and we must reap.
Brightest night brings gloomiest morning;—
   I must go, and thou must weep.

Weep, and view the world around thee,
   Through the tears that fall in vain,
As a landscape waste and dreary
   Through a window blurr'd with rain.

But the rain may cease ere evening,
   And the golden sun shine out,
And the landscape seem to blossom,
   Like a spirit freed from doubt.

Thou shalt find some flowers springing
   In the desert, here and there;
Thou shalt hear the sky-lark singing
   His sweet hymnal high in air.

Thou shalt find the world has solace,
    Even for sorrow like to thine,
That thy heart may beat for others,
    When it may not beat with mine.

Nay, my own, I do not doubt thee,
    For I know thy love is true;
But I know the world containeth
    Other hearts to love and woo:

And I would not thine should wither,
    Thine, my gentle Margaret,
Wedded to a love departed,
    Widow'd for a vain regret;

Clinging to the faded phantom
    Of affection changed and old,
As a mother clings despairing
    To her baby dead and cold.

Better thou forget me, dearest,
   As our lives are doom'd to part;
Absence heals the wounds of passion,
   Time may cure a broken heart.

And in after years, it may be,
   Though thou canst not all forget,
Thou shalt think of this our loving
   With a strange and sweet regret.

Thou shalt find thy heart new-waken'd
   By some old familiar song;
Find, perchance, some wither'd rose-leaves
   In a book forgotten long.

Faint and faded, like our passion,
   Once so fresh and dewy wet,
They in death shall own a fragrance
   That in dead love lingers yet.

Like the roses on a gravestone,
  Tended with religious care,
In the heart they wake the echoes
  Of the old love buried there.

As a traveller at evening,
  Gazing from a sunlit hill,
Sees some village loved in childhood,
  Where the rooks are cawing still;

When sweet voices of the children
  Float towards him on the breeze;
But the sobs he cannot stifle
  Are not half so sad as these.

Our two hearts have grown together,
  O my Margaret, all in vain:
They must soon be torn asunder,
  Like a mountain rent in twain:

When its wounded sides are beaten
By the tempest sweeping through,
So the world shall mock thy sorrows,
And thy wounds shall bleed anew.

Aye, but He who clothes the mountain
With a robe of ivy green,
Planting ferns and velvet mosses
Those uprooted rocks between,—

He shall heal thy wounds, my Margaret,
He shall bind thy bosom torn;
In His light thy griefs shall vanish,
As night phantoms flee the morn.

And in after years, it may be,
Thou and I may chance to meet,
With a smile of little meaning,
Though our hearts may quicker beat,

And our breath may catch a moment
   As we think of days gone by :—
But the world shall never know, love,
   What we once were, thou and I.

Fare thee well ;—the night is waning,
   And the morn must break the spell
That hath bound our hearts together :—
   O my Margaret, fare thee well.

TEARS.

FOND and foolish tears, that flow
Alike for pleasure and for sadness!
Is sorrow then a kind of gladness,
And pleasure but a phase of woe?

Or is it that a sorrow treads
Upon the heels of joy, and flings
Its shadow o'er the fairest things,
And blights the roses on their beds?—

And draws the clouds across the sun,
And saddens the gay world; and hushes
The April rapture of the thrushes,
And stills the robins, one by one;

And mingles with the children's speech;
   And folds itself our joys about;
   Until the mind is lost in doubt;
And cannot tell them each from each.

And when it thinks to lay its head
   On the warm breast of happiness,
   It shudders, for it seems to press
The wasted form of grief instead.

We must not weep for thoughts like these;
   For roses blossom on the tomb;
   And Spring is born of Winter's gloom,
And promise, of the leafless trees.

And, though at times some note of sorrow
   Should tremble from a heart unstrung,
   We need not weep, the world is young,
And big with many a glad to-morrow.

We may not weep for griefs that die ;
   We need not weep for joys that live :
   Yet tearful are the clouds that give
Its glory to the evening sky :

And richer are the tears that roll
   From those dear eyes, than I can count,
   Where I may drink, as at a fount,
And satisfy my longing soul.

O love, if love were more or less,
   We should not weep, for we should dwell
   In more than Heaven, or less than Hell,
And die of joy or weariness.

COME, dearest, for a while apart;
And I will tell my love to thee,
And thou shalt answer, love, to me,
And each shall read the other's heart.

Love is so precious in our eyes
We hide it from the sight of men,
And gaze upon it now and then,
As children on a cherish'd prize;

Or like two birds that build their nest
Deep in the half-fledged woods of spring;
And only dare their love to sing
When all the world is gone to rest.

And we have heard them singing thus,
   In some dark copse that hid the moon;
   And as they sang, our hearts kept tune,
Till half it seem'd they sang for us.

And watch'd the while the star of even,
   That waiteth till the sun shall die,
   To hang her golden lamp on high,
A link of light 'twixt earth and heaven;

And, when it shineth from above,
   Then lovers, with unconscious arts,
   Unlock the caskets of their hearts,
That hold the jewels of their love.

O love, this hidden love of ours
   Is like a garden hedged about,
   And shielded from the world without,
And stored within with choicest flowers;

Where thou and I may roam at will,
    And feed our senses with delight;
    And drink the honey'd dews of night,
And perfumes from the heathy hill.

And we have found beneath the trees
    Some tender flowers that love the shade,
    But in the sunshine droop and fade;
And thought our love was like to these.

And loved it better being thus,
    Than if it bloom'd in brightest day,
    With other flowers as glad and gay,
Sweet flower that only bloom'd for us.

PURE LOVE.

YES, dearest, we may love, and yet
We may not love as others do;
Our love must be both deep and
true,
Yet all unconscious of regret.

Yes, we may love, yet must we learn
To shield our love with jealous care
From thoughts that only bring despair,
And looks that pierce, and words that burn.

There may be, dearest, higher joys
In such untainted love as this
Than in the too tumultuous bliss
That with excess of sweetness cloys.

The sun is loveliest, when his rays
  Are veil'd behind a pearly screen
  Of summer cloud, that hangs between
Our sight and his too searching blaze.

And love is holiest, when enshrined
  Behind a veil of mystery;
  Thus will we worship him, nor pry
Too rashly at the god behind.

It may be, dearest, he would fall,
  Like Dagon, from his holy shrine;
  And what we worshipp'd as divine
Prove only human after all.

FORBIDDEN LOVE.

GOD, to live, and not to love!
  When love is sweeter far than life,
  That seems at best a weary strife
'Twixt heart and reason,—which may prove
The stronger—God, thou know'st, not I:
I can but dread the victory.

I may not love, yet must I live!
  My heart is tossèd to and fro;
  It may not cease, yet must not know
The joys that only love can give.
Yet oh, I dare not live alone—
It is not life, when love is gone.

Poor heart, 'tis like a lone sea-bird,
   That in the tempest seeks her nest,
   With aching wing and ruffled breast,
When nought is seen, and nought is heard
But angry sky, and angry sea—
There is no peace for her or me.

I may not love, yet strange it seems,
   That all my love, with all its madness
   Of sweet delight, and sweeter sadness,
Must fade away, like empty dreams ;
But, be the waking drear and chill,
They leave a lingering sweetness still.

I may not love—I must not die !
   Then let me dream my dreams again :
   My love has not been all in vain,
If I may live in memory.
For, though my sun of love be set,
Some twilight joys are left me yet.

Love was the child of my young heart—
   I could not bear to see it die;
   No, I will nurse it secretly,
And hold it to my breast apart;
And none shall know, not even he,
The joy my love is still to me.

Not even he, for I will borrow
   The world's unmeaning smile, and move,
   Bearing the burden of my love,
My love, so purified by sorrow,
That even he would hardly know
The passionate love of long ago.

But now and then, when none is by,
   I'll gaze upon my love, and weep,
   And rock it in my arms to sleep,
And clothe it in sweet memory;
And then for sterner tasks prepare,
The braver for the load I bear.

For sterner, holier tasks—to seek

   Some soul, more tempted and more sinning,

   And live again my life, in winning

My gentle sister, frail and weak;

And her unto the altar bring,

A most accepted offering.

.

So may I love! such love as this,

   So pure, and free from thought of sin,

   Will hallow the old love within,

And seem a foretaste of the bliss

That sainted spirits find in heaven,

Where tears are dried, and sins forgiven.

THE PURITAN'S DAUGHTER.

PART I.

THE sun was dying in state,
On a couch of orange and red;
Solemnly, like some pictured saint,
With the glory around his head.

And the clouds were gather'd about,
To watch their monarch die;
And we sat in the wood that autumn eve,
Together, my love and I.

Together, hand in hand,
In a newly-found delight,
Till the purple hills blush'd rosy red
In the kiss of the dying light.

Till it seem'd that the earth beneath,
   And the clouds in heaven above,
Were blent in a sea of golden light,
   A glory of hope and love.

Together, hand in hand,
   In the twilight calm and still,
Till the cold blue shadow was creeping up
   The side of the distant hill;

Till the chilly mist arose
   From the river that wander'd near,
Like the shapeless thing of a horrid dream,
   Or a vague, unmeaning fear.

Together, hand in hand,
   In the still and solemn night,
Till the moon came out of the eastern copse,
   With a red and angry light,

But paler grew, and sadder,
　As she rose in the violet sky,
Like a face on which some mortal woe
　Has fallen in times gone by.

Together, hand in hand,
　Till the thrushes awoke from sleep;
And my love was off to the wars to fight,
　And I went home to weep.

A fortnight past and gone,
　A fortnight sad and dreary!
And often I pray'd, and often wept,
　For my heart was lone and weary.

I prayed that they might not meet
　On the field of blood and strife,
My love, the lord of my heart and soul,
　And the father who gave me life.

For he was a Puritan, staunch
  As ever put hand to sword,
They had call'd him to lead a squadron of horse,
  Because of his zeal for the Lord.

But my love was a bold cavalier,
  And had follow'd Montrose, to fight
Against the Parliament rebels, he said,
  For the king and his sacred right.

And, O, I loved them both,
  But my father was stern and grim ;
And I knew my darling would not strike,
  If ever he met with him.

A fortnight past and gone,
  And I sat at the cottage door,
When I saw my father come back again,
  Grimy with dust and gore.

Weary, and wounded, and spent,
    But his eyes were all ablaze,
Ah me, how terribly changed he seem'd
    From the father of other days.

" Let us praise the Lord," he cried,
    " The Lord of power and might !
'Twas He that led our armies forth
    To the battle of yesternight !

" Let us praise him, O my child,
    The Lord of Hosts, for he,
With His own right hand, and His holy arm
    Hath gotten the victory.

" We smote them hip and thigh,
    And listen'd to no complaining ;
But the night came on as black as hell,
    We'd have left not one remaining.

" O, why wasn't Joshua there,
  To have made the sun stand still ?
The hours seem'd only too short, my child,
  But we hack'd away with a will.

" There was one, a comely youth,
  With love-locks, fair to see,
He had cut down many a godly saint,
  But he shrank from meeting me.

" Yet he would not turn and fly,
  So I slew him where he stood :
Look here, this tough old jerkin of mine
  Is splash'd with dainty blood.

" And I saw him take from his breast
  A locket of golden hair,
And he kiss'd it or ever he died; poor lad,
  He'd better have said a prayer."

That night, O God, that night!
  My father was gone to bed;
And I sat alone in my little room,
  Holding my bursting head.

I thought I was going mad,
  For I fancied that I could hear
The voice of my darling calling to me,
  Out of the darkness near.

Calling, calling, calling,
  In a voice so gentle and low,
That my heart grew sick of the love it bore,
  Grew sick of its love and woe.

" Let me go mad," I cried,
  " That so I may fondly deem
That only my love is true and real,
  And the rest is a ghastly dream.

" Let me go mad, my God,
 That so I may some time hear
The voice of my darling calling to me
 Out of the darkness near.

" Nay, but I am not mad,
 I am not mad or dreaming,
For there in the garden stands my love,
 With the moon-rays o'er him streaming.

" Wait for me, O my love,
 Where the autumn roses twine, .
For my heart is heavy without thee, dearest,
 It longeth to beat with thine."

Together, heart to heart,
 In the garden all that night !
And I kiss'd the blood from off his cheeks,
 In a passion of wild delight.

Together, lips to lips,
  Till the coming of morning gray;
And I was weeping for joy at home,
  And my love was hidden away.

He had been left on the field,
  Though his wound was slight, he said,
He had only fainted for loss of blood;—
  But a price was on his head.

At the back of the garden-wall,
  In an out-house crazy and old,
I hid the prize of my heart of hearts,
  As a miser hides his gold.

And every morn and eve,
  I brought him food to eat;
And the livelong hours I sat and thought
  Of the hour when we should meet.

And when it came, that hour
  Of joy unmix'd with sadness,
I was well-nigh wild for grief before,
  And now I was wild for gladness!

And oft in the silent nights,
  When the stars look'd down from above,
We walk'd in the forest hand in hand,
  And talk'd of our hope and love.

O days of hope and love!
  And of joy too great to bear!
Sure the sun was never so bright before,
  Nor the moon so wondrous fair.

Nor the diamond stars that trembled
  On the sable breast of night,
Nor the sober planets that sat and watch'd,
  Were ever so grand and bright!

L

Could they not linger on,
  Those days of a speechless bliss,
As dear as the first fond token of love,
  As sweet as the first fond kiss?

Could they not linger on?
  Why, as each morning pass'd,
O why did we feel, in our heart of hearts,
  'Twas a joy too deep to last?

Like the flush of a sudden pain,
  That thought came day by day,
O God, to have known such joy and love,
  .And to know they must pass away!

Why did I feel so sad,
  When I look'd at the sun-lit hill?
'Twas the thought of the cold blue shadow,
  And the white mist, colder still.

Why did I feel so sad,
  When I saw that mist again,
Tossing its arms in the wind, I thought,
  Like a spirit that writhes in pain?

Why did I shudder, and shrink
  From the breath of the autumn wind,
And the dropping leaves, that almost seem'd
  Like a footstep coming behind?

But again on my lover's breast,
  And all my fears had fled;
Yet why did he gaze with that wild, scared look
  At something over my head?

" What aileth thee, O my love,
  Why gaze at the open door?
Art weary of living for love and me,
  And wouldst thou be free once more?"

Ever the same scared look,
　　And still no word he said;
Till a vague, wild terror came over me,
　　A horror of doubt and dread.

I dared not look behind,
　　But I saw on the wall and floor
A shadow, that was not his nor mine,
　　From the light of the open door.

I knew it was come at last;
　　I felt that *he* was there—
My heart stood still, and my voice came thick,
　　As I utter'd a shriek or a prayer.

A cold hand on my arm,
　　And a face that I dared not meet!
I was grovelling down at my father's knees,
　　Clasping his great rough feet.

I clung with frantic strength,
　And cried to my love to flee;
" Away, away, for the love of Christ;
　Away, for my love, and me!"

My father trampled me down;
　But I clung with a maniac's strength;
Till my love, with a look that broke my heart,
　Was away in the night at length.

PART II.

THE winter had come, and gone,
　When I woke on my little bed,
　And saw my old nurse creeping about
With a soft and stealthy tread :

I heard the young birds singing
  In their nests in the bright sunshine;
But methought their song seem'd out of tune
  With a heart so heavy as mine.

My father enter'd, and spoke
  In a voice that was hollow and cold.
Sure years had past since I saw him last;
  He seem'd so haggard and old.

He motion'd the nurse to leave us,
  And sat in a vacant seat;
There burn'd a light in his cavernous eyes,
  A light that I fear'd to meet.

Still he never look'd at me,
  But murmur'd low to himself;
At length he arose from his seat, and took
  A bible from off the shelf.

He read of a Jewish woman,
  Who sat one day in the tent,
When a Syrian soldier pass'd that way,
  Weary, broken, and spent.

She rose, and ask'd him in,
  In accents gentle and mild;
And she wash'd his wounds, and chafed his limbs,
  As we nurse a wounded child:

But at night, when the stars awoke,
  And the guest was sleeping sound,
She put her hand to the workman's hammer,
  And nail'd him to the ground:

And she was a holy woman,
  And this her deed was blest;
For they who slaughter the foes of the Lord
  Are the people that serve Him best.

" But thou, that I call'd my daughter,
    Unworthy to bear the name,
Hast taken to thee of the cursed thing,
    And wrought thy father's shame ;

" And I, my God, and I,
    Who have bled for thy holy Kirk,
Have harbour'd a traitress here at home
    To undo the good work.

" 'Tis this that hath pierced my soul,
    As it were with a sword of steel,
And dealt me there a grisly wound,
    That nothing but death can heal.

" But enough of this.   I'm come
    To speak to thee of thyself."
And with that he placed the sacred book
    Again upon the shelf.

" Thou knowest the preacher here—
　A man of a godly life—
He hath ask'd of me these latter days
　To have thee for his wife.

" He knoweth of all my wrongs,
　And of all thy sin and shame;
But he knoweth too of my worldly goods,
　And he'll take thee all the same.

" Nay, dost thou start and shrink?
　Perchance thou hadst rather hear
Some news of that smooth-faced barber's block,
　Thy delicate cavalier?

" Well, I caught him some time since—
　He was lurking about the place;
And he's like enough to be hang'd ere long,
　In spite of his pretty face.

" But listen—no fainting now—
   (I see thou lovest him still!)
I have the power to hang that man,
   Or to spare him, as I will.

" If then thou wed the parson,
   Thou'lt save the neck of the layman;
But if thou refuse, by the God of heaven,
   He shall hang as high as Haman.

" Thou shalt have full time to choose,
   But mind me, and beware—
And I'll come again for thine answer, child,
   Soon after the evening prayer."

" My father, O my father!
   Nigh twenty years have fled
Since the angels took my mother away,
   And left me here instead.

" And thou used'st to love me well,
　For I've heard thee weep, and say
That God had not left thee desolate quite,
　When he took thy darling away.

" Thou wouldst place me on thy knee,
　As we sat at even alone,
And thou couldst not look in my eyes, my father,
　But a tear came into thine own.

" Thou must have loved her then
　With a love that was strong and true;
And now thou wilt break thy poor child's heart,
　My father, for I love too.

" I never knew my mother,
　But I know she was good and mild;
And I love to think she is listening now
　To the prayer of her poor lost child.

" My mother, O my mother,
  Would God thou wert here to-day!
I would kneel to thee on bended knees,
  And thou wouldst not turn away.

" O pity, and pray for me,
  From thy throne with the saints above!
For I was young and weak, mother,
  And I could not help my love."

My father heard no more,
  But turn'd and left me alone;
No longer to weep such bitter tears,
  For my heart was turn'd to stone.

I felt no sorrow now,
  But a burning sense of wrong;
And as my sorrow had made me weak,
  My anger had made me strong.

I would marry the man I loathed,
  To save my darling's life ;
But, though I were married a thousand times,
  I never would be his wife !

.

PART III.

AWAY, in a new strange land,
  A sad and silent land !
In a weary waste of water and wood
  Settled our pilgrim band.

By the side of a mighty river,
  That rolls its yellow stream
'Twixt endless forests that fold on fold,
  Stretch, like a weary dream.

A strange mysterious forest,
  With a silent, awful air !
No thrushes sang in their nests in Spring,
  No violets nestled there.

In a little shelter'd nook,
  Between the river and wood,
'Mid the blacken'd stumps of the giant trees,
  Our cluster of log huts stood.

And there, with four log walls
  From the bitter wind to screen us,
My husband and I, we dwelt together,
  With a gulf of hate between us.

A bridgeless gulf of hate,
  As cold as my changèd heart !
'Twas strange, two lives so near each other,
  Two souls so wide apart !

He was the village preacher,
  And every Sabbath day
The people came from far and near,
  To hear him preach and pray.

He preach'd a full, rich Gospel,
  And proved, with power of learning,
That papists, and other prelatical folk,
  Were only good for burning.

He told them that they, the elect,
  The chosen saints of the Lord,
Were to found a church in the desert land,
  To found it with bible and sword.

And the souls of the saints, he said,
  Must be white as the snow on Hermon!
But the more he'd tell of the pains of hell,
  The better they liked the sermon.

A bitter and gloomy race,
  With bible and sword in hand!
No maypole stood on the village green,
  As it used in the dear old land.

The women were hard and cold,
  With wonderful Hebrew names;
And even the children seldom laugh'd,
  And play'd at serious games.

My father was dead long since:
  I had sat and wept by his side.
I think he was sorry for what he'd done,
  For he bless'd me ere he died.

And a little while before,
  He told me he thought it best
We should go away with a pilgrim band
  To the new world in the West.

So there we dwelt together,
 In a log-hut, he and I,
With each a heart as cold and dull
 As the river that wander'd by.

We pass'd for a worthy couple,
 A model Puritan pair;
They call'd us the " godly man and wife,"
 Though all were godly there.

No sound in our hut was heard,
 Whether of wrath or laughter;
'Tis lovers who quarrel a moment now,
 To kiss the moment after.

Theirs is the summer sky,
 With its sunshine, shower, and cloud;
Ours the thick, snow-charged vapour, that wraps
 The dead earth like a shroud.

M

How I hated the life I led,
　And long'd for the moment when
I could flee to the great dark woods, and die,
　Or live with the wild red men !

I used to wander alone,
　By the lonely river's brink ;
There I could weep when none was by ;
　There I could weep, and think.

Think of the dear old days,
　When life was a dream of bliss—
What had I done, O God of heaven !
　For an agony like to this ?

I could weep to the solemn river,
　Or under some giant tree ;
But I could not weep in my husband's home,
　That home that was hell to me !

A bitter and gloomy race !
  With terrible oaths they swore
They would drive the heathen out of the land,
  As the Jews had done before.

With the bible in their mouth,
  And the broadsword in their hand,
They would sweep the cursed race, they said,
  From out the promised land.

They would slay, as Joshua did ;
  And listen to no complaints ;
For, " the earth was the Lord's, and all therein
  The heritage of his saints."

And 'twas true that the poor red man
  Knew neither to read nor think ;
And 'twas doubtless just to rob him, and kind
  To teach him to pray—and drink !

So backward, step by step,
   From their own wild woods they bore them
By force of arms, or cunning of guile,
   As the Jews had done before them.

But the poor red savage, who lack'd
   A Christian education,
Bore all his wrongs, I thought, with a most
   Unchristian resignation.

But, hearing our loud professions,
   And judging us from a distance, he
Wonder'd, perchance, if even the saints
   Could be guilty of inconsistency.

A quarrel arose at length
   About a portion of land,
('Twas the burial ground of the tribe, I think;)
   And the Indians made a stand.

So a battle was fought, that dyed
  The yellow river red ;—
And the listening forests heard a voice,
  As of women who wail for the dead.

They were only heathen women,
  So it didn't matter much.
The Christians call'd them " Philistines,"
  And shot them down as such.

I was sitting alone that night,
  By the log-fire dimly burning,
When I heard the tramp in the autumn leaves
  Of the Christian band returning.

They were singing a hymn of praise
  To the just and merciful Lord ;
Each with his smoking gun, I thought,
  Each with his reeking sword !

I was sitting alone that night,
　　Alone in the silent gloom ;
When a heavy hand was laid on the door,
　　And my husband enter'd the room.

He hung his match-lock up,
　　As he mutter'd his godly oaths ;
And he wiped the blood from his hands and face,
　　And the stains from his sword and clothes.

He said that the saints were to hold
　　A feast to the Lord that night ;
For that they had vanquish'd the foes of the Lord,
　　By the help of His arm of might.

I sate by the fire alone,
　　But neither to weep nor pray ;—
And I heard the saints as they drank full deep,
　　In a solemn, Puritan way.

At times a saint, or an elder
  Would hiccup a long oration,
With perhaps too many texts, I thought,
  And enough of self-laudation :

And the myriad stars look'd down,
  With their little innocent eyes,
On a scene so foul and brutal as this !
  On a banquet of murder and lies !

I sate by the fire alone,
  But neither to weep nor pray !
I was sick at heart of the life I led,
  And my thoughts were far away.

Away, in the dear old land,
  With my darling over the sea.
For in all my sorrows I loved to think
  That my love was thinking of me.

A heavy hand on the latch,
　And a heavy step at the door ;
And my husband's presence had dragg'd me back
　To my hated life once more.

He stood and glared at me,
　With a swaggering, drunken look,
I tried to answer him, glance for glance,
　But I felt that I trembled and shook.

So face to face together,
　In the silent gloom we stood ;
I felt the dread of a coming ill,
　And a horror that froze my blood.

My heart was dead within me,
　And my mouth was parch'd and dry ;
For the fatal hour was come at length,
　And I knew no aid was nigh !

" Thou'lt spoil thy pretty face
    With so much moping," he said ;
" Thou hast lost the roses from off thy cheeks,
    And thine eyes are swollen and red.

" Yet, still 'tis a dainty morsel,
    And fit for a godly saint !
Nay, I've a right to kiss thee, woman,
    And thou need'st not tremble or faint.

" I'm sick of thy sighs and tears,
    And thy scorn I'll bear no longer.
Nay, an we come to force, my beauty,
    Thou'lt find that I'm the stronger."

I sprang from his arms and seized
    A pistol from off the shelf :
" Back ! or I'll lay thee dead at my feet,
    And after I'll kill myself.

" Ay, I'll shoot thee dead, I tell thee,
   An thou venture a step too near ;
For the hour is come for me to speak,
   And the hour for thee to hear.

" Thou didst wed me two years since,
   And need'st not now be told
That it wasn't for love of my father's daughter,
   But for love of my father's gold.

" And I, when I married thee,
   To save another's life,
Had vow'd a vow in my heart of hearts
   That I never would be thy wife.

" His life, and my father's gold,
   Let each then keep to his own :
Thou art free to the money, but, by the Lord,
   'Twere wiser to leave me alone."

He laugh'd a brutal laugh,
   And snatch'd my weapon away:
" That pistol has never been loaded, fool,
   Since I fired it off to-day.

" I told thee a moment since
   That I'd bear thy scorn no more;"—
And with that he struck me a heavy blow,
   That flung me against the door.

My fall had burst it open,
   And there for a space I lay—
A moment—I sprang to my feet, and fled
   Into the night, and away.

PART IV.

DIE not, little stars,
   At the kiss of the dawn to-morrow;
For ye have brought me nothing but
      joy,
And the day may bring me sorrow.

" Die not, thou pale moon,
   At the birth of the lord of day;
For thou hast given me more than life,
   And the morrow may take it away.

" All day long I must crouch
   In the stem of a hollow tree;
But under the jewell'd breast of night
   I wander happy and free.

" So this is the river that roll'd
  Its mingled water and blood !
It looks as cold and cruel as man ;
  I'll back to my own wild wood.

" I love the dear wild wood,
  For there have my foes ne'er found me ;
Its leaves seem to whisper of hope, and its arms
  Are spread as a shield around me ;

" There I wander at will,
  All through the starlit hours,
And when I'm weary, I go to bed,
  And sleep with the strange wild flowers.

" Where the moss grows bright and green,
  On a grisly, wrinkled stem,
I've made me a pillow of fallen leaves,
  And I sing me to sleep with them.

" There I lie and sing,
    In the brown leaves nestling deep;
For I've made me a little song of my love,
    To sing myself to sleep.

Song.

" ' Alone in the wild wood,
    Here, over the sea,
I dream of my childhood,
    When first I knew thee.

" ' In the warm summer weather,
    And the bright morning hours,
We rambled together,
    And gather'd wild flowers.

" ' And often beneath, love,
    A wide-spreading tree,
Thou weaved'st a wreath, love,
    Of roses for me.

" ' But the leaves are the fairest
  When winter is nigh,
And our joy seem'd the dearest
  When ready to die.

" ' Now sad and alone, love,
  Here over the sea,
Still I'll think that my own love
  Is thinking of me.'

" Is this the morn that rises,
  Reddening the forest and flood ?
No, for the morn is violet gray,
  And this is crimson as blood !

" Now but a smouldering spark,
  An angry, blood-shot eye ;
It riseth now with a rush and roar
  That filleth the earth and sky.

" And a sound of rage and fighting,
  And cries of anguish and woe;
God !—do they come from the Christian village
  That I left but a night ago?

" What meant that madden'd shriek,
  That died in a piteous moan?
'Tis as if the devil with all his angels
  Were risen to claim his own.

" 'Tis the battle that rages again
  In all its foul deformity;
And the face of heaven is blushing red
  At the sight of man's enormity."

Deep in the leaves and flowers
  I buried my ears and eyes,
That I might not see that piteous sight,
  Nor hear those sickening cries.

Then I started up to my feet,
  And fled, I reck'd not where ;
For a horror and dread were over me,
  And a terror I could not bear.

Away, in the trackless forest,
  Alone, in the awful night,
For the moon had cover'd her scarèd face
  That she might not see that sight.

Whither—I cared not whither,
  Away from the smoke and flame ;
Away from the cries of fury and fear,
  And the deeds of blood and shame.

Whither—I reck'd not whither,
  My limbs were wounded and sore ;
But I fled, till the shining bark of the trees
  Was red with the flame no more.

N

Then I lay on the ground full weary,
  And with all my failing breath
I pray'd that God would give me soon
  His last, best gift of death.

" For indeed I'm very sad,
  Very sad and weary;
Death must be very sweet indeed,
  For life is very dreary.

" Weary, O so weary!
  Let me sleep and die.
Death must be very sweet indeed,
  To one so weary as I.

" O, death is very sweet,
  And this is a glorious place;
And the angel that bendeth over me now
  Weareth my darling's face.

" Speak softly and low, my angel,
  For fear that the charm should break ;
Or sing me a low, sweet angel song,
  And soothe me, lest I wake.

" Let me slumber on,
  With my angel's arms around me :
I know not whether 'tis earth or heaven ;
  But I know that my love hath found me ! "

(*He.*)

" Awake, my own, awake !
  Awake to my kisses and prayers !
Open thine eyes, my darling, and see,
  The daisies have open'd theirs.

" Arise, and smile on me,
  As thou smiled'st but now while sleeping ;
For the morning of joy hath arisen, and chased
  The long, long night of weeping.

" 'Tis well to have known such sorrow,
　For the joy that the morning giveth;
For my treasure was lost, and is found again,
　And my love that was dead yet liveth.

" Then awake, my own, awake,
　For the morning is changed into day;
And thy love is come, thy old, true love,
　To bear his darling away."

They lifted me up from the ground,
　In their arms so gentle and strong;
And they made a litter of boughs and leaves,
　To carry me gently along.

Through the cool, dark forest glades,
　And down to the shining river,
Where there waited a ship to bear us off,
　'Off and away for ever.—

Hand in hand on deck,
  Over the night waves dancing,
We watch'd the myriad stars of the sea
  Around the black ship glancing.

A wondrous night of stars,
  Of stars below and above !
And he told me of all he had suffer'd and done,
  Of all his sorrow and love !

How he had waited and watch'd
  Through the long, long months of sadness,
From the night we parted in anguish and woe,
  To the morning we met in gladness.

Of his dungeon gloomy and dark,
  Where never the sunlight shone ;
And how, when they gave him life, 'twas to know
  That the joy of his life was gone.

How, a changed and reckless man,
  He had sail'd to the Spanish main,
Seeking death in a hundred fights,
  But seeking it ever in vain ;

And how he was chosen at length
  The chief of a lawless band,
That long was known in the island seas,
  A terror to sea and land.

" But nerve thee, love," he said,
  " And keep thy hand in mine.
For I have a hideous tale to tell,
  Unfit for ears like thine.

" We had sail'd away to the north,
  For the crew was short of food,
And enter'd the river thou knowest well,
  In search of water and wood.

" Six days we had sail'd up stream,
   And the seventh night was o'er us,
When we sighted a column of smoke and flame
   Right in the wood before us.

" And out of the smoke and flame,
   But very faint and afar,
There issued Christian cries for mercy,
   And Indian screams of war.

" We ran our vessel ashore,
   And left her to fare without us,
And sprang to earth with matchlocks slung,
   And broadswords girt about us.

" But the wood was tangled and thick,
   And we made but sorry way,
And we enter'd the skirts of the village at last
   By the light of the morning grey.

" But nerve thee, O my darling,"
  Again he trembled, and said,
" I've seen the man that was once thy husband;
  God rest his soul, he's dead.

" At a bowshot from the village,
  By the side of a streamlet lying,
Clasping his broken broadsword still,
  Thy husband lay a-dying.

" His breath was failing fast,
  He knew he must die ere long;
And he told me in words that broke my heart
  Of all thy sorrow and wrong.

" Of all thy sorrow and wrong, dearest,
  And of all his sin and shame;
And how thou hadst fled the night before,
  That night the Indians came.

" They came at dead of night,
   Silent as death they came;
And the Christians buckled their armour on
   By the light of the ghastly flame.

" But all too late, too late,
   Whether to fight or fly;
The circle of red men hemm'd them in,
   And drove them back to die.

" All, all had fallen, he said,
   Children, women, and men!
He only was left to tell the tale,
   And he was dying then.

" We gave him water to drink,
   On a bed of leaves we laid him,
But, ere we could bind his wounded side,
   He was gone to the God that made him.

" We sought thee, love, in the wood,
   In the wood we sought and found thee;
With the golden sun on thy golden hair,
   And the wild birds watching round thee.

" A tear lay on thy cheek,
   For thou hadst slept while weeping,
Like a little pearl in its delicate shell,
   Or the dew in a snow-drop sleeping.

" We watch'd my darling sleep,
   Those golden morning hours,
Like a little weary bird in his nest,
   On her pillow of leaves and flowers.

" Then I woke her—ay, I woke her,
   With such a passionate kiss,
I would have died for a kiss like that,
   And now I have lived for this!"

In the quiet old village church,

The parson read the banns ;

We had knelt at God's high altar before,

And now we knelt at man's.

And I thought, when all was o'er,

And the ring and the blessing given,

It may be marriage is made on earth,

And love is born in heaven.

THE LAST NIGHT.

THE rain is dripping drearily
  From the boughs of the leafless
    trees;
And the wind is sighing wearily
  Like a spirit that's ill at ease;

And the timid birds are nestling
  In the depths of the ivy screen;
And the great elm boughs are wrestling
  With the might of a foe unseen;

The poor little love-sick flowers
  Have cried themselves to sleep:
And oh, these long night hours!
  And O God! that I could weep.

The wanton clouds are snatching
　Kisses from the scarèd moon :　.
And oh, I am sick of watching,
　I shall die if he come not soon.

Hark, how the night-wind sigheth ;
　And the windows shudder and start :
Oh, a burden of sorrow lieth,
　Like a cold hand, on my heart.

For my joy is turn'd to sorrow,
　As the gloom hath cover'd the light ;
I shall die ere morn to-morrow,
　If my darling come not to-night.

'Tis the light that shineth brightest,
　The deepest shadow throws ;
And, O love, thou unitest
　The deepest joys and woes.

They never have joy'd so madly,
   Who never have learn'd to sigh ;
They never have mourn'd so sadly,
   Who never have loved as I.

Yet, O God, I would live to press him
   To the heart that he taught to beat ;
Live—were it but to bless him
   For the love that made life so sweet.

Even here, in my desolation,
   Forced from my darling apart,
I can think of the revelation
   Of love to my poor heart.

'Twas a morning bright and holy,
   And we wander'd hand in hand,
Watching the wavelets slowly
   Come creeping over the sand.

The wondrous light lay sleeping
  On the sea and the golden beach ;
And the little waves were peeping
  On tip-toe, each over each ;

And clapping their hands with laughter,
  As they danced in the morning sun,
And fell in homage after
  At the feet of my darling one.

Some simple love-words merely,
  He whisper'd me softly, and I—
O God, I loved him dearly,
  Madly, I knew not why.

He promised that he would love me,
  And swore that the throbbing sea,
And the sun in the blue above me
  Were not more true than he.

And I—oh, I could not doubt him,
  Believing was too much bliss;
So I flung my arms about him,
  And clung to him with a kiss.

How could my darling part from me
  After that fatal day?
Why did he win my heart from me,
  Only to fling it away?

'Twas cruel thus to deceive me,
  So feeble, and he so strong;
Cruel in grief to leave me,
  Who never had done him wrong.

On a little grave, where only,
  Only a dead hope lieth,
Sweet memory bloometh lonely,
  A flower that never dieth.

It needeth not tears even
　To water it, but hath still
Through tearless sorrows thriven,
　And while I live, it will.

Listen, the birds are waking,
　And singing ;—what care they
That a heart, more or less, is breaking?
　It happens every day.

Soon shall the dew-drops glisten,
　And the skylark chaunt on high,
Till the wondering earth shall listen
　To his passionate minstrelsy ;

And the gallant sun shall sweetly
　Kiss from her forehead brown
The dew-tears she so meetly
　Had shed, when he went down ;

And the violet and primrose blossoms,
Adown in the woody dell,
Shall bare their maiden bosoms
To the sun that they love so well.

But, over the daisy meadows,
And along the primrose lane,
And down in the beechen shadows,
I shall never ramble again.

My playmates perhaps will miss me,
A short while, when I'm dead ;
And my darling will come and kiss me,
Here on my little bed.

I would not live to reprove him
With my poor broken heart,
But just to say how I love him
Once more before we part.

It may not be.—Ere to-morrow
  This weary life will cease ;
This life, where love is sorrow,
  For another, where love is peace.

THE MAIDEN AND THE LILIES.

LEAVE thy lilies, gentle maid,
　　Here are jewels rare;
　Gold and jewels thou shalt braid
In thy golden hair.

" Jewels live when lilies die,
　　True love dieth never;
　Flowers shall wither by and by,
　　Gems shall last for ever."

Then she took his jewels bright,
　　(When did maiden reason?)
　Dreaming of a strange delight
　　For a summer season.

But, ere spring-time came again,
Faithless love departed.
Faded were her lilies then ;
She was broken-hearted.

LOVE AND DEATH.

SHOULD the sun, like gallant knight,
  Wooing some gentle, timorous
      maiden,
Kiss with his lips of light
Some little delicate bud, dew-laden.

The bud shall blossom and bloom,
For love is the light her young heart needeth ;
  And the maiden shall meet her doom,
And follow her love where'er he leadeth.

But the flower shall droop, and sigh
Her odorous breath to the blast that chilleth ;
  And the woman shall weep and die,
For she hath loved with a love that killeth.

What though her love be death?
Better to die than live to doubt it;
For sweeter sure, she saith,
Is death with love, than life without it.

SONG.

YOU have waken'd the old love that
 was sleeping
 O my dearest, in my heart;
I had soothed it to slumber with much weeping,
 When our paths had seem'd to part.

You have waken'd the old love, as the showers
 Wake the meadows to delight;
As the first ray of morning wakes the flowers
 That were sleeping through the night.

You have waken'd the old love, and to-morrow
 We shall love and mourn again.
For with love, O my dearest, cometh sorrow,
 And with passion cometh pain.

THE PORTRAIT.

ER hair was a golden brown;
   The photograph makes it black:
You may take the picture out if you
   like,
You'll find a lock at the back.

And her eyes were a living blue;
   And, through their splendour rare,
You could gaze right into her soul, and see
   The passions that sported there.

Why did we part? God knows.
   It may be that she and I
Love still with as true and tender a love
   As we swore in the days gone by.

To see a mighty rift
In a mountain, who would think
It was rent in twain by a tiny rill,
That had trickled in at a chink?

Needs but an angry thought,
Or a light word lightly spoken,
And a mountain of love may be rent in twain,
And the chain of life be broken.

You may solder it up if you will,
But the place will always show;
It's better to do as she and I,
Far better to let it go.

DOUBT.

FAIR, sweet face! and can it be
    That thou art but a lying mask?
God knows! thou still art dear to me,
And more than this I dare not ask.

I will not rob me of my bliss,
    But think thee true as thou art fair.
Better to dream such dream as this,
    Than wake, if waking brings despair.

MORE DOUBTS.

CAN falsehood lurk in form like thine?
Can those blue eyes, that should
be true,
And that dear heart, that beat with mine,
Beam love, and throb for others too?

I dare not ask, I will not stir;
I can but wish, if this could be,
If true, that I might live for her,
If false, that she were dead for me.

OLD LOVE LETTERS.

DEAR relics, that I must destroy ;
As though my heart could thus
forget
That once ye made it leap for joy,
And make it throb for sorrow yet.

Dear little notes! some mystic power
Still tells me what was lurking there,
That this one sent a bud or flower,
And this one held a lock of hair.

I clung to you, when all was gone,
The last young bird to leave the nest.
My heart is empty now, and lone,
For ye must go, like all the rest.

S when a great oak dieth, that in life
Hath drunk up all the virtue of the
soil,

Leaving it barren—so my love is dead,

That drank up all the love-springs in my heart,

So that no other love may grow therein.

Oh, it were better, like some stunted flower,

That never breathed the warm breath of the sun,

Ne'er to have breathed the perfumed breath of
love.

So bitter is it to have " loved and lost."

SONG IN SORROW.

SING to me, O my love,
    For my heart is heavy within me.
    Sing to me, O my love,
    Sweet music, that may win me
From the gloomy demon of thought,
    That firm in his arms hath wound me.
Sing, till thy voice hath wrought, hath wrought
    Its rapturous spell around me.

Sing me of gallant knights,
    That whisper'd in ladies' bowers ;
Or sing me of breezy heights
    Of purple and golden flowers ;

Where the stately forests listen
　　To the monotone chaunt of the sea;
And the heath-bell wakes, and her tear-drops
　　　glisten,
　　As she yields her sweets to the bee.

Or sing me a fairy tale,
　　Some foolish wild romance;
How at night, in the moonbeams pale,
　　The fairies meet and dance;
Marking with tiny rings
　　Their haunts in the woodland dells;
And hurrying home, when the skylark sings,
　　To sleep in the fox-glove cells.

Or sing me of paynim giant,
　　And of lady with golden hair,
On her own true love reliant,
　　That his arm will save her there;

Or of high-born damsel, keeping
  Her watch in lonely tower;
Or of love-lorn maiden, a-weeping, weeping,
  Like hare-bell after a shower.

Or sing me a solemn strain;
  And tell how the heroes die,
When over the trampled plain
  The bleeding warriors lie;
Or sing of the angel band,
  From home and friends departed,
The wounded to nurse with tenderest hand,
  And to comfort the broken-hearted.
      '

Or sing me of all thou art,
  My treasure, my joy, my own;
Sing, till my beating heart
  Keep time with thy tremulous tone.

Sing, till thy lustrous eyes
    With diamond tear-drops shine ;
Sing, till the voice of my soul arise,
    And mingle, and die with thine.

LOVE.

AN'S soul is like a ship, that in the
night
Towards some fatal shore
Is drifting more and more,
No pilot there to guide her course aright;
And those old charts that once had power to
save
From rocks, and shoals of doubt,
That lie her course about,
No longer trusted; but the wilful wave
Sports with her for awhile, and drags her to the
grave.

O love, thou art the haven of the soul!
And to thy beacon's spark
We steer our labouring bark,

For there is peace, when angry billows roll;

There, in thy sheltering bosom we may lie;

And, safe from every gale,

Repair each shatter'd sail,

And hear the hungry surges sweeping by,

Where gentlest ripples play, and softest breezes

sigh.

There the glad sun is shining all day long;

While in the woody vales

Full-throated nightingales

Do make the air to tremble with their song.

And there the stray dove that hath lost his nest,

Beneath thy sheltering shore

Shall fear the storm no more,

But smooth the ruffled plumage of his breast,

And fold his weary wing, and sleep, and be at

rest.

And there the queenly moon, at close of day,
    Doth from her silver crown
    Scatter the jewels down
Upon the heaving bosom of the bay;
While, through the silent watches of the night,
    The amorous summer breeze
    Doth woo the sleeping trees
With softest whispers, and with kisses light,
Till all their leaves awake to tremulous delight.

Yet are there some, who linger there awhile,
    And shield them from the storm
    Within thy bosom warm ;
But should the heaven look bright, and ocean
    smile,
They launch once more upon the treacherous
    main ;
    To quench in busy marts
    The fire of their young hearts ;

And, when in age they seek thee, 'tis in vain :
Of them that left thee once thou art not found
　　again.

And some there are who scorn thy choicest
　　treasures ;
　　And steal the fruits and flowers
　　That deck thy fragrant bowers,
To waste in vain delights and idle pleasures.
But all their sweets shall turn to bitterness ;
　　For ev'n thy grapes let fall
　　Not wine, but bitter gall,
When hands unhallow'd do their juices press ;
And thou art found a curse, that most hast power
　　to bless.

And there are some, who seek thee painfully,
　　With sighs, and bitter tears,
　　In youth, and riper years,
To rest them for a little ere they die ;

Oh, not for them the perfumed branches wave
 Above the golden beach
 That tiny ripples reach;
But all alone the joyless sea they brave,
Until they find at length the shelter of the grave.

Love, thou art sweetest in the early spring;
 When in thy rocky dells
 Are violets and bluebells,
And honeysuckles climb, and thrushes sing;
And all the earth is wet with early showers,
 When even the sun appears,
 As shining through his tears,
And there are tears within the blushing flowers,
And tears of love are shed in thy delicious bowers.

And when in Summer, blinded by the heat,
 And weary with the oar,
 We seek thy kindly shore,
Even then, O love, thou hast a welcome sweet,

There we may rest upon some mossy root;
And all our cares forget,
Where beauty lingers yet,
And vernal bloom is changed to summer's
fruit,
And roses blossom still, though nightingales are
mute.

Then cometh winter, when the nights are
dreary;
And all the sleepless trees
Moan to the bitter breeze,
And toss their bony arms, as they were
weary;
Then only they who in the spring did come
May find a shelter still
From northern tempest chill,
All else upon the ruthless ocean roam,
Their only haven death, the grave their only
home.

O love, my spring is over, and the flowers
    Have wither'd one by one,
    And now the summer sun
Hath driven all the birds to sheltering bowers.
The nightingales are silent, yet the lark
    Still to the morning sky
    Poureth sweet melody,
And still thy beacon shineth through the dark,
A kind and welcome light to my benighted bark.

Oh, may I reach thee ere the winter blast
    Sweep o'er the surging sea,
    In blackest terror free,
And split the sail, and snap the trembling mast.
I may have slighted thee in spring, when o'er
    The ocean's heaving breast
    The breezes sank to rest,
And lazy ripples crept along the shore :
Oh, may I reach thee now, I will not leave thee
    more.

CONVENT THOUGHTS.

UNDER the cypress-trees,
  That stand in order stately and tall,
  Gazing over the convent wall,
And drinking the evening breeze,
That bloweth over the Arno vale,
A nun was seated, haggard and pale,
  And uttering thoughts like these.

Oh, a weary fate !
Dragging the tedious days along,
With matins, and compline, and evensong,
  And vigils early and late ;
Or a walk in the convent garden trim
With the lady abbess, stately and prim ;
  I that could love, or hate !

Oh, a weary time !
Here in the convent, alone, alone,
Wearily, wearily making moan !
Oh, that I could climb
Into the cypress-branches, and gaze
On the valley that lies in a golden haze,
With its belts of cedar and lime !

Better I could not hear
Voices that come to me over the hill,
When the sun goes down, and the air is still,
Ringing so joyous and clear ;
Voices from vineyard and olive grove,
Of laughter and song, and whisper of love,
A sound so strangely dear.

Better I had not heard
Those two young lovers whispering near me,
So near, I dreaded lest they should hear me,
As I drank in every word ;

Till my heart beat quick with fancied blisses,
And my cheeks burnt hot with fancied kisses,
    And all my blood was stirr'd.

    And then when they ceased, and I
Heard not the night-bird's passionate singing,
Nor the convent-bell in the turret ringing,
    But each fond word and sigh
A voice in my heart was still repeating,
With every pulse still wildly beating,
    With the thoughts that would not die.

    Why was I born to miss
The passions that other women know,
The joy of loving, or even the woe
    That cometh of too much bliss?
For an hour of such sweet joy and sorrow,
Of tears to-day, and smiles to-morrow,
    I would give up a life like this.

Had I but known the charm
Of a true love, I could have yielded
My soul unto him, who would have shielded
    His darling from all harm;
Then, in each doubt and tribulation,
His love had been my consolation,
    My confidence, his arm.

One hour of love were worth
Whole years of a life like this, one hour
Would gladden my heart, as a summer shower
    Gladdens the parchèd earth.
It would cheer me even when sad and old
As the year looks back, when the nights are cold,
    To the spring, and the violets' birth.

None ever loved in vain:
Even when love is unrequited,
And hope is dead, and the heart is blighted,
    Sweet thoughts will still remain:

And the memory of some kind, loving word,
In the silent night-time faintly heard,
  Will soothe a life-long pain.

  Love is more prized and dear
Than is our life, for love shall never
Die with our death, but live for ever,
  Though all forgotten here.
All have loved once, even she who seems
The loneliest, wakens, perchance, in dreams,
  Some love in a far-off sphere.

  Surely such love must be all
A sweet devotion, calm and high,
For such is the soul in its extasy!
  Alas that such pure ideal
May soothe, though it cannot satisfy.
Oh, I must love, or I shall die,
  A love that is human and real.

Surely my heart speaks truly,

When it tells me of unknown joys and sweets,

And of vague delights, till it beats, it beats,

With vagrant thoughts unruly,

That I try to stifle in vain, in vain!

The petals cannot be closed again,

When the flower is open'd newly.

I cannot but love, not I,

Even as the lark must soar in heaven,

And the nightingale sing in the woods at even,

And the great sun shine in the sky;

As the eye must see, and the tongue must speak,

My heart must love, or it will break!

Must love, or I shall die!

Alas, that it cannot be!

No—I must back to tell my beads,

I can only think when no one heeds,

And sorrow when none may see :

And then to my cell till break of day,

To try to sleep, and to try to pray,

Oh, so wearily, wearily !

THE ECHO IN THE BAPTISTERY OF PISA.

STRIKE those notes again,
In the same slow measure,
For they woke a pain,
Mingled so with pleasure,
I would count them o'er like a miser's treasure.

As a golden dream,
When the sleeper waketh,
In the morning's beam
Still sweet music maketh,
Soft, and very sweet, like distant sea that
breaketh.

Q

Even so come stealing,
In those simple notes,
Thoughts of vaulted ceiling,
Where the music floats,
Most marvellous and sweet, as from young angel
throats.

Angel voices calling
From the marble dome,
Rising now and falling
Harmonised they come,
Like voices heard in dreams of half-forgotten
home.

Listen how the single
Notes that she and I
Utter, meet and mingle,
And make harmony,
Like souls divided here, that meet again on high;

Purified, descending,

Freed from earthly leaven,

Like the praises blending

Over sins forgiven,

When simple tones of earth are glorified in
heaven.

.

Sweet is memory, bringing

Thoughts of happier days,

Coming back, and singing

Snatches of old lays,

Until the heart is lost in most delicious maze.

Like the scent, that clingeth

Unto roses dead;

Like a child that bringeth

Flowers to grace the head

Of a cherish'd form, when the soul is fled:

So, o'er heart that droopeth,

Old with wasted powers,

Childlike memory stoopeth,

Bringing, in sad hours,

Far-off voices faint, and scents of faded flowers.

A FRAGMENT.

 SIT at a window smoking,
   High over a seething street,
   Where the tall black houses echo
The fall of a thousand feet.

And the crowd, like a sightless giant,
   Beneath me staggers and reels,
To the hum of a thousand voices,
   And the crash of a thousand wheels.

And a thousand eager faces,
   Alike of the young and old,
Hurrying hither and thither,
   In the frenzied fight for gold.

And over the world are atoms
As eager and fierce as these;
Climbing over each other,
Like mites in a mouldy cheese;

And over the world there echoes
The selfsame feverish cry—
" Let me but gather a heap
Of guineas before I die!"

Strange—for no gold can purchase
A moment of life or health;
But the poor man dies in his poverty,
And the rich man dies in his wealth;

And the work-house buries the poor,
While the bones of the noble and rich
Are swaddled in silks and velvets,
Like butterflies drown'd in a ditch.

Yet still they pick up money
 At the price of honour and blood ;
And the poor man pockets with thanks
 The halfpenny flung in the mud ;

And the rich, to be richer still,
 Will flatter, and cringe, and lie !
Is it only to ride in state
 In a plume-deck'd hearse when he die ?

Bah ! the moral is stàle,
 Stale, and the dullest know it ;
And to rave at the wealth he covets
 Is the rôle of the hungry poet.

Nay, but is death ennobled
 By an army of mutes in scarves ?
And is life made better or happier
 By coaches and footmen's calves ?

Surely the prize is paltry,
  Be it ever so nobly won;
Sure labour is better than wealth,
  As a legacy left to a son.

Better the mine of diamonds
  Than a jewel, though costly and bright;
Better the sun in heaven
  Than gas or electric light;

Better than letters or music
  Is the man that speaks and sings;
And better is honest labour
  Than the money that labour brings.

Let us work and live for to-day;
  He's better who scribbles or digs
Than the wretch who hoards his money,
  Or spends it in flunkies and gigs.

Let us work and live for to-day,
　And the morrow shall shift for itself ;—
Ere the morrow shall dawn—who knows ?
　The urn may be laid on its shelf.

" Nay, but I work for my children,
　I toil for the babes I rear ;.
My son, sir, shall sit in parliament,
　My daughter shall marry a peer ;

" And I shall have founded a family "—
　" Nay, then, 'twere hard to reproach
The father who drives a barrow
　That his children may ride in a coach."

Yet fame were a nobler object
　To work for, early and late ;
Though fame is only a pillory,
　Where the little fling mud at the great.

HORACE.

Second Epode.

BLEST is he who lives contented
On the fields his fathers rented,
Like the men who lived and labour'd
in the happy days of old!
Not for him the usurer's treasures,
Not for him the city's pleasures,
While his oxen plough the acres that his fathers
loved to hold.

Careless, though the battle's thunder
Wake to glory, blood, and plunder;
Careless, though the ocean rages, and the angry
billows roar,

Careless, though the mart be teeming
With its speculators scheming ;
Careless, though the crowd be cringing at the
  proud patrician's door.

But he loves the wild vine flinging
Tender branches fondly clinging,
In the chaste embrace of wedlock, to the poplar
  high and pale ;
And to hear the cattle lowing
By the rivers gently flowing,
Where the mountains rise in glory round his own
  ancestral vale.

Or amid his fruits to linger,
Graft and prune with careful finger ;
Or to cull the fragrant honey from the hollow
  trees and rocks ;

Or his gentle aid to render

To the young lambs weak and tender,

Or to shear the heavy fleeces from the mountain-

roaming flocks.

Or, when autumn, fair and blushing,

Rich in apples ripe and gushing,

Heralds plenty o'er the valleys with a smile and

with a nod,

Then his luscious pears he musters,

With the vine's purpureal clusters,

And he lays them with a blessing on the altar of

his god.

Praising the benignant powers,

Guardians of his fruits and flowers,

Soft reclining 'neath the branches, weaving gar-

lands over-head;

Lying in a dreamy slumber,

While the doves their sorrows number,

And the streamlet prattles idly with the pebbles

in its bed.

Then, when winter snows are falling,

Dogs˙and men about him calling,

He with arts and arms primeval tracks the wild-

boar to his lair;

Spreads his nets in brakes and bushes

For the fruit-devouring thrushes,

Or displays, with mighty boasting, crafty crane

or timid hare.

Who could feel his spirit blighted

With affection unrequited,

With a frugal wife to meet him, when his daily

work is done ?—

Such as Sabine hills excel in ;

Such as dark-hair'd maidens, dwelling

Where the parch'd Apulian mountains glow

    beneath a southern sun.

Thanks to her the logs are burning

For her simple lord's returning ;

She it is that milks the kine, and leads them to the

    well-known stall ;

She the fragrant cask that broaches

As his welcome step approaches ;

She that cheers the frugal banquet with a smile

    of love for all.

Not the shell-fish, sweetest daughter

Of Lucrinus' crystal water ;

Not the turbot, pure as snow-flake, not the rosy-

    tinted char,

(Should the winds in wild commotion,

Lowering o'er the eastern ocean,

Kindly waft to Roman tables strangers welcome

as they are ;)

Not the bird from Afric's mountains,

Not the quail from Hellé's fountains,

With a flavour more delicious could my hungry

belly fill,

Than the fragrant berry shining

'Mid the olive branches twining ;

Or the wholesome dock, or mallow, dress'd with

her sweet woman's skill.

Then how sweet the festal morning

Of great Terminus returning,

When the lamb and kid are slaughter'd for the

banquet of the day,

Sweet the frugal master's pleasure,

As he counts his bleating treasure

Hastening homeward from the pastures by the

old accustom'd way.

Sweet to view the cattle trooping,

With their languid heads down-drooping,

As they drag the plough inverted, slowly winding

o'er the lea:

And his troop of servants, which is

Such a sign of household riches,

Ranged around the polish'd lares. O how happy,

they and he !

Thus old Alphius ends his singing,

And aside his ledger flinging,

Swears he'll cut the broker's business, and be off

to wood and wold;

But a tempting speculation

D——s his sage determination,

And the calends find the poet more a usurer than

of old.

A MAGDALEN.

THE sunlight was slanting
  Through purple and red;
And the white-robed were chanting
  The prayers for the dead;

The organ was pealing
  From pavement to roof;
And a woman was kneeling
  And weeping aloof.

Aloof, and dejected,
  Alone, and forlorn!
Her garment, neglected,
  Was draggled and torn.

The rich ones pass'd by her,
  Their proud steps she felt;
But no one came nigh her,
  Where lowly she knelt.

They shrank from her raiment,
  As though from pollution;
They came with the payment
  That claims absolution.

O surely unkindly
  They shrank from her touch!
She had loved but too blindly,
  And trusted too much.

If the sinful thus hate her,
  And spurn her away,
Can her sinless Creator
  Be gentler than they?

But God that is holy,
From out of the crowd
Had chosen the lowly,
Rejecting the proud ;

So the merchant and banker
Had paid, and were shriven ;
But her sins, that were ranker,
Were purged and forgiven.

THE ARTIST'S CHILD.

TAKE him away from the palette, my
    Willie, my darling one !
    Take him away from the palette, and
  bid him gambol and run,
Or sport with the neighbours' children, or bask
  in the noonday sun.

God keep him from being a genius ! I'd choose
  him to dig or sweep ;
Or out in the purple meadows with his brothers
  to sow and reap,
Or deep in the earth to labour, like ant in an
  earthy heap.

God keep him from being a poet, from dreaming
    of things too high ;
From seeing a golden vision, to wake to the
    children's cry,
When they cry to their father for bread, and he
    may not make reply.

Take him away from the palette, darling, and
    teach him to plough ;
And to eat, like Adam of old, his bread of the
    sweat of his brow.
God, had they left me thus, I might have been
    happy now !

But the foolish, gossiping neighbours, as soon as
    the work was o'er,
And the silent shadows crept from the mountains
    over the moor,
Wonder'd and gazed at the figures I chalk'd on
    the cottage door.

" Ah, the boy is a genius, too good for the plough
    or the loom !"
So they sent me off to the city, to paint in a dismal
    room,
That I peopled with ghostly figures, as the twilight
    died in the gloom.

So I painted my first great picture, and made my
    first success ;
And took thee, Mary dearest, to wife ; for how
    could I guess
That the morning of joy must die in a night of
    bitterness ?

And then our Mary was born, our child with the
    violet eyes,
Deep and tender and true, as the dying light in
    the skies,
Our darling, who under the turf in the far-off
    churchyard lies.

And then our troubles began ; for Mary was ailing
and weak,

And we carried her down to the sea for awhile,
but ere she could speak,

The angels took her away ; and we thought our
hearts would break.

Oh, it's hard to work for fame, but harder to work
for bread,

When the heart is, oh so weary, and the hand is
heavy as lead,

And the eyes are dim with crying for a little child
that is dead.

But the critics praised my work, though the
patrons wouldn't buy ;

They said my painting was sad, my art was gloomy
and high ;

" Give to us something cheerful and light," so
I said that I'd try.

Cheerful and light ! O God, or ever the grass had
    grown
On the little mound of earth; or the woodbine
    had cover'd the stone,
Where our tiny flower with the violet eyes was
    sleeping alone !

I might have known I should fail; and I fail'd,
    and had to bear
The smile of pitying praise, that's worse than an
    honest sneer ;
And that with the doctor's bill, and the studio rent
    in arrear !

Oh then the weary struggle, the weary struggle
    and strife !
Anything paltry and mean that would bring me
    bread for my wife !
I cared no more for art, but I cared for my
    darlings' life.

I cringed to the critics and dealers, and ask'd them
to come and dine,
And praised their vapid wit, and their daughters
vulgar and fine ;
And they came, and ate my dinners, and sneer'd
at my painting and wine.

It fail'd, Mary, it fail'd, and I'm broken-hearted
at last.
I dare not look to the future ; and I'm mad when
I think of the past ;
And the hand of death is on me, Mary, I'm dying
fast.

You'll be better off when I'm gone, dearest, for
they'll be kind to you then.
God! how sorrow has changed me, for you
remember me when
I wouldn't have left my darlings to the mercy of
other men.

But poverty stifles pride, love, poverty stifles
   pride!
Now I must leave you to God, and maybe He
   will provide
Something for you and Willie, dearest, when I
   shall have died.

But take him away from the palette, Mary, and
   teach him to plough;
And to eat, like Adam of old, his bread of the
   sweat of his brow.
Anything better than dying as I am dying now.

THE STARLING.

ENTLE, kindly starling,
That bringeth to his darling,
With kisses and fondest whisperings,
Worms, and other delicate things,
That, out with the old, hoarse-throated rooks,
He findeth in fragrant furrow'd nooks;
And percheth on her cage,
Her captive grief to assuage
With plenty of cheery chatterings.
There's a touch of sorrow in all he sings;
Like the smile, that again and again
I've seen on a gentle woman's lips,
When tears have wetted her eyelash tips,
The angel-smile, that all in vain
Would stifle a sudden sob of pain.

Gentle, loving starling!

O that my own darling

Could fly from her home away, away!

   With a love as tender and true as thine;

   And whisper, and nestle her breast to mine,

And tell me half that she longs to say.

I would sit in my dungeon all day long,

      And listen at night

      For her footstep light,

And the passionate notes of her throbbing song

And she'd press her delicate lips to the bars,

      And kiss me through,

      As the starlings do,

And be, oh so happy, under the stars!

TO THE MEMORY OF A PAINTER.

E is gone, he, the brave and single-
hearted !
Where his old friends have buried
him, he lies ;
And another great spirit is departed,
To receive, sure, his guerdon in the skies.

Though the hand had grown weaker and more
weakly,
Still the brave man labour'd at his art ;
But the wrong he had learn'd to bear so meekly,
Though it couldn't make him murmur, broke
his heart.

He is gone where the mighty ones are humbled ;

He is gone with his honour, and his pride,

He had stood where the mighty ones have

stumbled ;

But he couldn't learn to pander, so he died.

But the widow he hath left here to languish,

Let her joy that the bitterness is past ;

For if here he found sorrow and great anguish,

Surely there he is comforted at last.

ONLY.

ONLY a woman's face,
　　In the dark night and cold;
　　But oh the ghost of a vanish'd grace,
And the pitiful tale it told!

Wrapp'd in a ragged shawl,
　　(Why was it not her shroud?)
It look'd as white as the moon at night,
　　Through a rift in a driving cloud.

Only a few pence,
　　And a few kind words addressing;
And all they brought was a grateful thought,
　　And a poor lost woman's blessing!

SAN MINIATO.

ERE'S a little sketch I made,
   While my darling gather'd flowers,
And we wander'd in the shade
   That the ancient walls and towers

Flung across the peopled plain,
   And the Arno seaward creeping;
Like to death that without pain
   Passeth o'er a maiden sleeping.

Oh how often she and I,
   When my painter's work was done,
From the crested convent nigh
   Watch'd the death-scene of the sun.

S

Watch'd him dying lone and grand,
Lone and sad he seem'd to us.
" We will die, love, hand in hand !
Death were surely sweeter thus.

" Die ! 'tis but to sleep for ever,
Lip to lip, and heart to heart !
What hath death that it should sever
Those whom life hath fail'd to part ?

" See, the widow'd Earth is turning
To the pale face of the moon.
Cold are now those glances burning,
Loved too dearly, lost too soon.

" See, she dons her robe of sorrow,
Weeping tears of sweetest dew,
He shall rise again to-morrow,
And her love be born anew.

" Listen, dearest, to the sighing
    Of the cypress, low and sweet ;
And the murmur, never dying,
    Of the city at our feet.

" Every passion, every feeling,
    Songs of love and cries of fear,
Harmonized hy distance, stealing,
    Make a strange, sweet music here.

" See, the golden moon is steering
    Proudly up the purple skies ;
See, one little star is peering
    Down with half-awaken'd eyes.

" I could linger here reclining,
    Seeing nothing far and wide,
But the stars above me shining,
    And my darling by my side.

" With our hearts together beating,

    Breathing your delicious breath ;

And our lips in kisses meeting,

    I could languish unto death.

" But the city lights are gleaming

    Through the white mist at our feet.

We have had enough of dreaming:

    One more kiss, love, long and sweet;

" And to-morrow we will wander

    By the streamlet you may see,

Gleaming in the moonlight yonder,

    Underneath Fiésole."

MARGARET. A RETROSPECT.

PART I.

ERE it is, the dear old garden,
  Wasted now, but lovely yet;
  With its borders weed-encumber'd,
And its alleys green and wet.

Still some roses bloom neglected,
  Still some woodbine-tendrils wave,
Sadly sweet, as daisy blossoms
  On a poor, neglected grave.

Still the old armorial bearings
  Stand in melancholy state,
Like the pride that flaunts in tatters
  On the ruin'd entrance-gate.

You remember how I sketch'd it,
   With its guardian figures grim ;
And the stately elms that border'd
   The broad alley, swept and trim ;

Half concealing the tall gables,
   And the gray and wrinkled tower,
Where the pigeons ever circled,
   And the clock clang'd out the hour ;

And the portal, rose-embower'd,
   Where the porter, worthy soul,
To the gentry gave admittance,
   And to beggars gave a dole.

And the mullion'd window, peering
   Through the grizzled ivy boughs,
Like the eye of some old giant
   From beneath his shaggy brows ;

And the hall with roof of timber,
   And high windows richly dight :
And the quaint and curious armour,
   Never used since Worcester fight ;

And the stiff ancestral portraits,
   Shepherd ladies fair and slim,
Statesmen looking wise and solemn,
   Warriors looking bold and grim.

And the spacious oaken staircase,
   And the chamber long and dark ;
And the chapel of St. Herbert,
   'Mid the beeches in the park.

Ruin now, and desolation
   Both in hall and chapel reign,
Broken are the twisted chimnies,
   Rusted is the gilded vane ;

Silent the old clock, while o'er it
  Ivy tendrils trail and climb.
But the brave old race departed,
  What have they to do with time ?

Here too all my hopes were blighted,
  Like those rosebuds on their stem ;
Here my heart was changed by sorrow,
  As the frost hath wither'd them.

Fittest scene for saddest musing ;
  Here then will we sit and think,
Here uncoil the chain of memory,
  Thought by thought, and link by link.

It was twenty years last April,
  When we left the smoky town,
With its endless crowd and bustle,
  And its houses dull and brown.

We were sick of the old study,
 Where the plaster walls display'd
Yards of canvas, all discolor'd
 With effects of light and shade.

Where I sketch'd chaotic fancies,
 Never doom'd to see the light ;
While you plann'd the famous system
 That should set the world aright ;

Where we forged the bolts of thunder,
 Heralds of the coming storm,
That should work the grand Millennium
 Of our socialist Reform.

You would lead the world to Wisdom,
 By appeals to head and heart ;
I would raise it up to Virtue
 By the aid of lofty art.

We would sweep the mouldy systems
　To the limbo whence they are—
Tremble, parsons, in your pulpits !
　Tremble, lawyers, at the bar !

But the parsons and the lawyers
　Pass'd unconscious by the door,
Heedless of the shafts we fashion'd
　On our dingy second-floor.

Well, we laugh at these illusions,
　That the world has put to rout,
Now our hands have learn'd to tremble,
　And our hearts have learn'd to doubt.

But the world is changing round us,
　Men no longer drink and fight,
Settling in the cool of morning
　Drunken quarrels made at night.

Thieves no more are hang'd for stealing;
  Wayside gibbets stand no more,
Bearing rows of rotting corpses,
  Like the rats on stable door;

And our fathers, could we see them,
  We should deem them rude and strange;
For the world is changing round us,
  Though not we have wrought the change.

Not the poet in his closet,
  But the craftsman at his trade;
Not the painter with his palette,
  But the navvy, with his spade.

Yes, the man of thews and sinews;
  Then, when he has clear'd the way,
Comes the preacher with his sermon,
  Comes the poet with his lay.

Thus the finer spirits finish
    What the stronger arms began ;
And a road lies through the desert,
    Levell'd for the march of man.

Well, I said, we left the city,
    Weary of its dust and noise,
Weary of its fruitless labours,
    Weary of its fruitless joys ;

Weary of our student orgies,
    With their waste of wit and wine ;
Weary of our loves, forgetting
    Each in turn had seem'd divine.

Left the town, and pass'd the suburbs,
    Where the villas stand in ranks ;
Till we found the primrose blossoms
    Growing in the daisy banks ;

Till we saw the young corn springing
  In the fields to left and right,
Heard by day the thrushes singing,
  And the nightingales by night.

And our hearts, awaken'd newly,
  Drank in every sight and sound,
As a child's heart wakes, and wonders
  At the glories spread around.

You remember how we wander'd
  Through the woods, and by the rills,
And where hamlets nestle snugly
  In the hollows of the hills.

How I sketch'd the feudal castles,
  Bringing back the olden time;
How you learn'd the ancient legends,
  Learn'd, and shaped them into rhyme.

How you sang of opening blossoms,
  Call'd them maidens young and coy,
Longing, trembling yet to open
  All their hearts to love and joy.

How we talked of love and friendship,
  Though of love we knew no more
Than know children of the ocean,
  That have sported on the shore ;

For the foolish love-caprices
  Of our boyhood were as far
From a true and living passion,
  As a marsh-light from a star.

" Love," we sang, " is like the blossom,
  Breathing perfume from the lime ;
Blooming in the summer season,
  Dying in the winter time ;

" Friendship, like the solemn fir-tree,
   Rooted in the moorland bare.
When the leaves are dead and fallen,
   Then the robins shelter there.

" Love is like a wayward streamlet,
   Coming down from rocky hill ;
Now a fierce, destructive torrent,
   Now a tiny, plashing rill ;

" Friendship, like a placid river,
   Flowing on through valleys wide,
Ships and barges heavy laden
   Bearing on its ample tide.

" Love is like a comet, blinding
   With its strange and sudden light ;
Friendship like the pole-star, guiding
   Watchful seamen night by night."

Thus we chatted in our wisdom,
　Measuring in our tiny span
All the deep, mysterious workings
　Of the inmost soul of man.

'Twas the first and sad reaction
　In the mind that sought the light ;
That had swept the ghosts and fairies
　Of its childhood out of sight.

Gone the tales of paynim giants,
　Knights and ladies ; gone, in sooth,
Lessons sweet of matchless courage,
　Deathless love, and spotless truth.

'Twas the spirit waking sadly
　From its childhood's golden dreams ;
When its world of fruits and flowers
　But a wasted desert seems.

'Twas the first, cold doubt arising,
  Like a snow-cloud, chill and dense;
'Twas the mustering of the forces,
  For the fight of faith and sense.

Later on, when sense has brought us
  Weary heart, and aching brain,
Comes the banish'd faith of childhood,
  With its joy and peace again ;

Then the old man gathers sadly
  What the youth hath cast away,
Tottering home with feeble footsteps,
  Never more to doubt or stray.

It was evening, you remember,
  When we reach'd the craggy brow,
Where the oaks, and silver beeches
  Slept in sunset, then as now.

We were tired of painful climbing
Up the mountain's further side,
In the mighty shadow, stretching
O'er the landscape far and wide:

And we gladly reached the summit,
Gladly, on the rugged crest,
Deep among the ferns and mosses,
Flung us down to gaze and rest.

For the sun was setting slowly,
Underneath the western sky,
Glaring on the beauty round him
With his eager, dying eye:

And the valley lay beneath us,
Sleeping in a purple shade:
And the thrushes trill'd a welcome
Out of every glen and glade.

And the beeches seem'd to murmur
  To the gentle summer breeze,
While the river mourn'd responsive
  To the murmur of the trees.

We could see it toss'd and fretted
  Into many a foamy wreath,
Through a maze of tangled branches,
  In the dark glen, far beneath :

And beyond it lay the Castle,
  Flank'd with limes and mighty elms,
Seeming like some monarch hoary,
  Gazing on his feudal realms.

And, still further, lay the village,
  In the shadow of the church ;
And the thrushes sang a welcome,
  In the woods of oak and birch.

Oh, the wondrous, wondrous beauty !
Oh, the calm delicious hour,
Coming back, through years of sadness,
With a strange and mystic power !

Like the face of dear companion,
Loved and lost in early life,
Coming back, like angel vision,
In a world of doubt and strife !

But the sun was dying, dying,
Like a king upon his bed ;
And the golden-tissued curtains
Closed in splendour round his head.

Then we rose, and left the mountain,
Climbing down from ridge to ridge,
Down to where the river flashes
Underneath the granite bridge :

Till we reach'd the " Golden Dragon,"
    Shelter'd by its ancient oak ;
Where, beneath the choral branches,
    Village worthies sit and smoke.

There we rested, eating gladly
    Of the hostel's homely fare ;
Then, on beds that smelt of heather,
    Slept, till song-birds woke the air.

Part II.

THESE two trees, that whisper o'er us,
    Whose fond branches twine and
        wreathe,
Where the robins love to nestle,
    And soft summer winds to breathe—

These we planted here together,
　She and I, one Autumn morn;
Tender vows and burning kisses
　Spoke our love, when they were born.

'Twas a foolish fancy, doubtless;
　We were foolish then and fond:
Love had spread a glory round us,
　And we could not look beyond.

Nay, perhaps 'twas truest wisdom,
　This our folly, that could bring
Higher good than sages dream of,
　In the love that poets sing.

Well, we sat, and watch'd the shadows
　Creeping o'er the velvet lawn,
Creeping o'er the timid daisies,
　Pale as lingering stars at dawn.

And she bent her head, and whisper'd,
  In her soft and gentle speech,
" Let us plant two trees together,
  Let us bend them each to each.

" They shall grow a living token
  Of our love from day to day ;
As our hearts have grown together,
  Oh, my dearest, so shall they."

Then we planted them together,
  In the garden side by side ;
And they grew, and flourish'd greatly ;
  Throwing branches high and wide ;

Twining fondly round each other,
  Bough to bough, and stem to stem :
And our hearts had grown together,
  Mine and Margaret's, like to them.

Oh, my Margaret! how I loved her,
   From the morn I saw her pass,
With a bunch of golden cowslip,
   Gather'd in the jewell'd grass.

I was sketching the old gateway;
   And I watch'd her sweet surprise,
As she stood and wonder'd at me,
   With her large mysterious eyes.

But I made as though I saw not;
   For I long'd that she should stay,
And I fear'd my gaze would scare her,
   Like a timid fawn, away.

Then she crept on tiptoe nearer,
   Like a robin hardly tamed,
With her little mouth half open,
   Blushing, as though half ashamed.

Still I made as though I saw not,
  But I watch'd her none the less;
Till I heard her frighten'd breathing,
  And the rustling of her dress;

Then I rose, as if to greet her;
  But she blush'd a deeper red;
Blush'd, and, scarce a glance bestowing,
  Through the beeches turn'd and fled:

And I watch'd her fleeting figure
  With the deep, enraptured gaze
Of a saint, who sees a vision
  Of a glory, as he prays.

And I waited, long'd, and waited,
  But she came not back again;
And my heart was beating strangely,
  With a dull, unmeaning pain.

It could hardly be I loved her,
  Who had never named her name ;
But her going left me lonelier
  Than I had been ere she came.

So a golden beam of sunlight,
  Streaming through an open door,
Dies, and leaves a lonely chamber
  Sadder, lonelier than before.

So the skylark's hymn at morning,
  After every throbbing close,
Fills the air with deeper stillness
  Than before the music rose.

You remember, that same evening,
  As we stroll'd upon the green,
How I told you all the story
  Of the vision I had seen.

How I seized my paints and brushes ;
  Vowing I would die, or trace
Something of her woman's beauty,
  Something of her childlike grace ;

Something of her deep blue eyes, and
  Something of her tresses brown,
That, beneath her garden bonnet,
  Fell in wavelike masses down ;

Floating like some angel pinion,
  That the breeze of morning stirs,
Though I doubt if angel ever
  Own'd a foot so small as hers.

Then you laugh'd and said, " Some other
  Angel should you chance to meet,
Where will be this angel vision,
  With its hair and tiny feet ?

" Come, I leave this place to-morrow,
    For a letter came to-day
Calling me to other duties,
    That no longer brook delay.

" And I warrant, ere a fortnight
    You'll have ceased to think of her,
And have found some other angel,
    She, some other worshipper."

But I would not, so you left me,
    Left, and took your Kate to wife;
And we both have floated downward
    On the crowded stream of life;

Floated, each on divers currents
    That have met again at last;
Each, a link that binds the other
    To the dreamland of the past.

You would weary, did I tell you
   All our love, and how it grew
From a foolish, passing fancy,
   To a passion deep and true.

For, alas, the seed of love was
   Sown upon a virgin soil;
And the tree had grown and blossom'd,
   And the roots had, coil by coil,

Wound about our hearts, or ever
   We had thought of danger near;
For we never dream'd our fondness
   Was a passion we should fear.

But one evening, late in summer,
   I and Margaret walk'd alone
On the terrace, where the lichen
   Gilds the quaintly carvèd stone.

And I spoke. My voice, it may be,
  Trembled, though I knew not why:
" I am going—I must leave you ;
  And I'm come to say good bye.

" And to thank you and your father
  For the kindness you have shown
Unto one who came among you
  Uninvited, and unknown.

" And I've brought you, as a token
  Of my gratitude, the view
That I sketch'd of the old gateway,
  That same morn I met with you."

So I gave it ; but she trembled,
  And her face grew white, and flush'd,
Then our eyes met ; and my passion,
  Like a sudden torrent, rush'd

Up from out my soul, and issued
  In exceeding bitter cry.
" O my Margaret, hear me, hear me !
  I must speak, or I shall die !

" I have loved you, oh so dearly,
  Since the day I saw you first ;
And have chain'd my tongue to silence,
  When my heart was like to burst.

" Nay, I know there lies between us
  A great gulf, a social sea—
That I cannot rise to you, love,
  And you may not stoop to me.

" And I'd sworn to kill this folly,
  Though my heart should die as well ;
Or at least to love in silence,
  Though such silence seem'd a hell.

" Nay, you must not blame me, dearest,
  For a love so deep and true.
As the daisies love the sunshine,
  So my heart must worship you."

Then she answer'd very sadly,
  With a face as white as stone,
" O God, help me, for I love you !
  And my life is not my own.

" Leave me, leave me, O my dearest,
  For I dare not tell you all ;
Come to-morrow, in the twilight,
  Underneath the orchard wall."

So she left me, watching, watching,
  While the moon arose on high,
Trampling out the stars that met her,
  In her triumph through the sky.

And my passions raged within me,
  Like the fiend that haunted Saul;
But a mighty exultation
  Rose triumphant o'er them all.

" Margaret loves me ! yes, she loves me ¦
  Surely it were well to gain
Such a love, and die to-morrow ;
  Should I thus have lived in vain ?

" Margaret loves me ! So will I, then,
  Like the stately moon above,
Trample down the social barriers
  That would keep me from my love."

Then arose the chill reaction,
  Stealing over brain and heart—
" Fool, that pratest in thy folly !
  Think of her and what thou art.

" Thou, a paltry, nameless painter,
　　Is it well that thou aspire
To a child of proudest lineage,
　　Daughter of a Norman sire ?

" He that gave thee kindest welcome,
　　Bade thee in his halls to stay ;
Thou, that camest, and hast stolen
　　His sweet Margaret's heart away.

" Is it well ?"　And then I answer'd,
　　" It is well that I have done—
Man would keep our hearts asunder,
　　God hath will'd that they be one.

" What are fashion and convention ?
　　Bastard offspring of to-day !
Love is Godborn, and eternal,
　　And it shall not pass away !

" As the firmament is wider
  Than a suckling infant's span,
So the law of God is holier
  Than an ordinance of man."

To the orchard in the twilight,
  Came I back to watch and wait ;
Where the chestnuts, turning golden,
  Shade the ivy-crested gate ;

And I saw her come towards me ;
  And I thought my heart would burst :
And we clasp'd our hands together,
  Though we neither spoke at first.

But we stood, and gazed a moment,
  Each into the other's face ;
Then our hot lips clung together,
  In a passionate embrace.

And we did as other lovers,
 Who at twilight meet and kiss;
Sighs, and whispers incoherent,
 Made the sum of all our bliss.

But we thought ourselves in heaven;
 And no doubt 'twas sweet to sip,
As a bee from summer roses,
 Honey from her rosy lip;

And to clasp my Margaret to me,
 Closer, closer, more and more,
Till our two hearts beat together,
 As our souls were one before.

But across her face a sorrow
 Pass'd, like cloud across the sun;
And the tear-drops trickled slowly
 From her eyelids, one by one.

Then I pray'd, with thousand kisses,
　By our passion deep and true,
She would tell me all her sorrow,
　That my heart might sorrow too.

But she answer'd, crying wildly,
　" Not to-night, oh, not to-night !
Love me now, but hide the future,
　Hide it, dearest, out of sight !

" Were it well to talk of sorrow,
　Love, on such a night as this ?"
Then she seal'd my lips to silence
　With a long, long, throbbing kiss.

And the while the stars were watching,
　With the stately planets seven,
Like the eyes of loving angels,
　Peering through the chinks of heaven.

And the moon was sailing slowly,
　　Through the firmament on high,
Like a ship 'mid starry islands,
　　In the ocean of the sky.

But a voice was calling " Margaret,"
　　In the garden far and near;
And she knew it was her father,
　　And she paled and shook for fear;

As an aspen pales and shivers
　　When it feels the thunder blast;
When the sun that wont to cheer it
　　From the tempest shrinks aghast.

" One more kiss, and I must leave you,
　　Love, to dream of strange delight!
Meet me at this hour to-morrow—
　　Yet another, now, good night."

So the summer changed to autumn ;
  And I met her day by day ;
And she told me all her sorrow,
  And I kiss'd her tears away.

But I found it was a sorrow
  Even kisses fail'd to cure,
Such that she, with all the solace
  Of her love, could scarce endure.

" Many years ago," she told me,
  " I, as yet a thoughtless girl,
Was affianced by my father
  To the grandson of an earl.

" So the world proclaim'd us lovers,
  And we bow'd us to our fate ;
Meeting with a calm indifference
  That was neither love nor hate.

" And perhaps I thought I loved him ;
    For indeed I never knew
More of love than such indifference,
    Till the day I met with you.

" And he's coming here to claim me,
    Claim me, dearest, for his wife ;·
And I'd rather die than meet him ;
    Better death than such a life ! "

Then I answer'd very sadly,
    Kissing her imperial brow,
" Two ways lie before you, Margaret,
    You must choose between them now.

" One would lead you up to splendid
    Halls of well-nigh princely state,
Where the world would spread before you
    All it owns of rich and great ;

" You would reign a queen of fashion,
Dukes would deem a priceless prize
Just a rosebud from your bouquet,
Or a smile from those blue eyes ;

" And the other, lower, lower,
To a level not your own ;
Where you might in deepest sorrow
Reap the harvest you had sown.

" Love and poverty, too often,
Are the parents of regret ;
While the marriage-bed feels softer
Underneath a coronet.

" Yes, 'tis true, though unromantic—
What, you shake your head in doubt ?
Herbs, with love, you think are better
Than a stallèd ox without.

" But, remember, that was written
　By a king in all his pride ;
He'd have told a different story,
　May be, Margaret, had he tried.

" Could you leave without a murmur,
　All the world for such as I ?
Are you sure that you would never
　Chide me with a look or sigh ?"

Then she answer'd, " Do you doubt me ?
　Have I given my heart in vain ?
I have pour'd my love upon you,
　Would you yield it back again ?

" Think you, love is like the roses,
　That in shadow lose their bloom ?
Love is like a lamp, that shineth
　Brightest, in the deepest gloom.

" Do not doubt me, do not doubt me !
    For indeed my love is true ; .
And you'll find that I can welcome
    Want and sorrow, all, for you."

And I said, " Then God forgive me,
    Darling, if I do you ill—
Will you go with me to-morrow ?"
    And she wept and said, " I will."

Then we seal'd our loving compact
    With fond kisses long and sweet—
Vowing we would love each other
    Till our hearts should cease to beat.

But she started, white with terror,
    For a shadow cross'd the path ;
And her father stood before us,
    All his " visage changed " with wrath.

But he smiled, and speaking slowly,
   Said in accents low and clear :—
" You must pardon this intrusion,
   But I knew not you were here.

" And it may be I'm old-fashion'd,
   But I deem it hardly right,
I should find my Margaret lying
   In the arms of such a knight ;

" She, affianced to another,
   Worthy of her house and name !
Nay, it seems you think as I do,
   For I see you blush for shame.

" And this gentleman, your lover,
   Thinks, no doubt, as well he may,
Running off with such an heiress
   Were a scheme that ought to pay.

" True, the lady would be ruin'd,
    As she'd merit well to be ;
But her father could but give her
    What were wealth for such as he.

" Truly, 'twas a gallant project ;
    But 'twill fail, I greatly fear.
And, allow me, sir, to mention
    That when first I ask'd you here,

" 'Twas to paint my dogs and horses,
    Not my daughter's lips to kiss.
Never did my young ambition
    Rise to such a height as this.

" But, if you could kindly spare her,
    'Twould perhaps be just as well ;
As her other lover's coming,
    And her swollen eyes might tell

" More than would be quite convenient ;
   And 'twill soon be time to dine."
But she nestled closer to me,
   With her tearful face in mine.

" Do not strike him, O my darling,
   Do not strike him, for my sake ! "
Then she ceased, and for a moment
   Wept as if her heart would break.

Then, " May God forgive you, father,
   For you do him foulest wrong."
But his fury burst its barriers,
   Like a torrent damm'd too long.

" Must I send the men, to tear you
   From your paramour's embrace ?
Must I send the lacqueys here, and
   Bid them drag him from the place ? "

PART III.

ALL was over ! Life no longer
    Held a prize I cared to win.
All the world was changed without me,
All my heart was changed within.

Calm they deem'd me, unimpassion'd ;
    'Twas at times when none was there,
That the love that burn'd within me
    Seem'd a grief I could not bear.

So, when all the earth is blooming,
    With fair flowers and purple heath,
Bursts a fierce volcano, showing
    Something lives and burns beneath.

I had lived at Rome and Florence,
  Learning little that was good;
Sear'd and harden'd, and I knew it,
  Try to hide it as I would.

I had friends, for I had money;
  Gain'd them both at dice and loo—
Men of spotless honour, doubtless,
  Ready to defend it too.

Honest? Well, they lied to women,
  And sometimes, at sorest need,
Left their tailors unrequited;
  But, in their too simple creed,

Virtue was a thing, that ladies
  Wear in public, like a glove;
Men were born to lose at billiards,
  Women, women—well, to love!

Margaret.

I had gain'd a reputation
  With the gossips of the town,
Having fought a famous duel
  With a swordsman of renown.

'Twas about a certain countess,
  That I ran the baron through.
I believe he really liked her;
  As for me, I hardly knew.

I had loved so many women,
  Of such varied hues and nations,
Loving seem'd like ever playing
  One old air with variations.

This one was a Tuscan countess,
  With black eyes and glossy hair,
And a husband, so they told me,
  Living cheap in Le'ster Square.

He had held some foolish notions
   Of advancement of his kind;
So they'd bow'd him from the country;
   But his lady stay'd behind.

She, in politics, was tory,
   Staunch as was the ducal press.
While, in morals—well, in morals
   She was liberal, I confess.

At the Pergola I met her,
   Where she eyed me in my stall;
Then in the Cascine; thirdly,
   At the Grand Duke's fancy ball.

Where we danced too much together;
   So at least the baron thought;
Which, as he was then her lover,
   Much displeased him, and we fought.

Did he think to kill a rival ?—

" L'homme propose et Dieu dispose."

What a tale the Florence quidnuncs

   Learn'd next morning, when they rose !

Fallen was the mighty baron,

   Prince of swordsmen, who till then

Was esteem'd a young Achilles,

   Loved of women, fear'd of men.

Fallen on the field of honour,

   Kill'd, at first the gossips said.

True, at length he did recover,

   But he spent a year in bed.

So, in place of killing me, 'twas

   He was laid upon the shelf.

I, while he was starved and blister'd,

   Had the countess to myself :

When, a fortnight spent in Florence,
    And a winter pass'd at Nice,
Fann'd to something like a passion
    What was once a mere caprice.

Passion ! well, we gave each other
    All of love we had to give.
You may galvanize a body,
    But you cannot make it live.

So, for want of something better,
    In a dead heart you may still
Galvanize the corpse of love, and
    Call it loving if you will. . . .

Shall I tell you how I met her,
    Met my Margaret once again ?
Married, with the earl, her husband—
    How she saw me, and in vain

Strove to hide her burning blushes,
  And the pallor cold as death,
And the trembling of her fingers,
  And the catching of her breath?

How we met with feign'd indifference;
  Never, by a look or sigh,
Spoke the words we burn'd to utter,
  Or the thoughts that would not die.

Met, as others meet, till no one,
  Of the crowds that went and came,
Dream'd the embers smoulder'd in us,
  That a word might fan to flame:

Till each almost thought the passion
  Dead within the other's breast;
Oh, it was not dead but sleeping;
  Would that we had let it rest!

But one day, I call'd and found her
  Weeping in her room alone,
And I spoke, and call'd her, Margaret,
  In the old familiar tone :

And she raised her tearful face, her
  Poor white face, so sad and sweet,
That I could not speak for sorrow,
  But I flung me at her feet.

Kneeling for a moment only,
  With my arms about her there,
For a moment, while her fingers
  Twisted idly in my hair ;

And the lips that sought each other,
  Hot, and wet with blinding tears,
Clinging for a moment only.
  Then she rose, as one that hears

Margaret.

Toll the death-knell of a lover;
  And in words that seem'd to thrill
All my soul with all their sorrow,
  " Leave me, dearest, say you will !

" God knows that I love you dearly,
  If you love me, do not stay :
Let me dare to love my darling
  In my prayers by night and day.

" If you call me, I shall follow,
  Though you lead me to remorse ;
Though the love, that was my blessing,
  You should change it to my curse.

" Do not call me, do not call me !
  For my love, before you came,
Was the dear old love of girlhood,
  Free from thought of sin or shame.

" I will pray for you and bless you,
   If you leave me : should you stay,
I shall love you, God forgive me,
   But I shall not dare to pray."

Then I answer'd, " I will leave you,
   One more kiss, and now, good-bye."
And she murmur'd, " God will bless you,
   O my darling, as will I."

So we parted, and for ever !
   She, before the year was done,
Died of what they call'd consumption,
   I had wander'd on and on,

Over lands and over oceans :
   I must work, so people said ;
Work is but an idle labour,
   When the thoughts are with the dead. . . .

And the place is gone to ruin,
    While they settle hostile claims ;
And the world has quite forgotten
    What were once such honour'd names ;

But the poor have not forgotten,
    After well-nigh twenty years,
Who it was that smooth'd their pillows,
    Who it was that dried their tears.

Somewhere in a cypress-garden,
    Underneath the crested steep
Of a quaint Italian city,
    Gentle Margaret lies asleep.

She was only twenty-five, yet
    Look at these two locks of hair,
One a golden brown, the other
    Lined with silver here and there.

THE SHRINE BY THE WAYSIDE.

IT stands beside the beaten way;
　　And there the market-women rest,
　　And make the sign upon the breast,
And lay their burdens down and pray.

And tens of thousands, like to these,
　　Have knelt to that unchanging face,
　　And worn a little hollow place
In the hard granite, with their knees.

And one, whose child is sick to death,
　　Will weep and pray the livelong hours;
　　And bring a wreath of early flowers,
A violet or primrose wreath,

And hang it up and go her way,
  With less of anguish in her soul;
  And one that is but just made whole
Of some sad sickness, ere she pray,

Will hang the crutch she needs no more,
  Or some rude print, or waxen limb;
  And offer up her thanks to Him
Who made the lame to walk of yore.

And yet 'tis but a simple shrine,
  And holds a form of rudest art,
  A woman with a bleeding heart,
A woman with a child divine.

What then? It is not rude to them,
  To that poor mother, blind with tears,
  The tinsel crown the Virgin wears
Is more than monarch's diadem.

'Tis only that they need a sign,
　　To see the greater in the less ;
　　And by the simple form express
Some higher truth, and more divine.

'Tis Superstition, if you will,
　　That sees a beauty not its own
　　In painted wood, and carvèd stone ;
And plants the cross on every hill ;

And robes the priest in silk and gold ;
　　And swings the incense till it rise
　　In clouds about the sacrifice :
But Superstition came of old,

An erring child of holy race ;
　　And, wandering at her wayward will,
　　The child of Faith, she weareth still
Some likeness of her mother's face.

And, in the night of unbelief,
  Some souls her beacon light shall bless,
  That guides them through the wilderness,
Though but a fitful light, and brief.

They need a symbol.   As a lover
  Wears at his heart, when far away,
  The image of his love, so they,
Poor simple loving souls, discover

In humblest forms of wood and stone
  The image of their Lord ; and feel
  A joy beneath the cross to kneel,
For love of One that hung thereon.

What then ? 'tis nothing after all.
  A superstition worn to shreds.
  It cannot stand where Reason treads.
We must have Reason.   Let it fall.

And, tried by such a test as this,
   'Twould fall, it may be ; who can tell ?
   But, lest it drag down Faith as well,
'Twere wise to leave it as it is.

Reason and Faith must dwell apart.
   To Reason's eyesight Faith is blind.
   Reason sits thronèd in the mind,
But Faith lies nestled in the heart.

There nestled, like a brooding dove ;
   But dovelike too, she soars on high,
   Where boasted Reason cannot fly,
To meet her heaven-born sister, Love.

Yet fades she in the icy breath
   Of Reason, as the buds in May
   Die of late frosts ; so hearts decay,
Faithless, unloving to their death.

What then? Must Error flourish long,
  Lest Faith should perish in its fall?
  Better to know no faith at all
Than one that bolsters up a wrong.

But who is he, in very sooth,
  Who, seeing with his reason's sight,
  Saith, Thou art wrong, and I am right,
Or, That is error, this is truth?

For, " What is truth?" No answer came,
  When Pilate ask'd the Jews of old.
  Now age on age hath o'er us roll'd,
And left the question still the same.

We seek it as an alchemist
  Sought for the stone that turns to gold.
  And who shall say, The truth I hold,
And I will preach it as I list.

Yet are there trusting souls and meek;
　To whom their faith is joy indeed;
　Who glory in the simple creed,
That speaks alike to strong and weak;

That saith, beside the open grave,
　That in their death must life begin,
　That love alone a crown shall win
From One that only waits to save.

And who shall steal their faith away,
　Their little store of joy and hope,
　Their little strength wherewith to cope
With the world's trials, day by day?

And who shall say their simple prayer
　Is one that God will fail to own?
　And who shall cast their idol down?
He cannot place another there.

And with their faith might chance to fall
  Their joy on earth, their hope of bliss,
  Better the heart that loves amiss,
Than one that " never loved at all."

And though some mists of error screen
  Aught of Truth's sunlight from their gaze,
  Mayhap they love the transient rays
The rather for the clouds between.

We know not who the seed hath cast,
  And may not reap, who cannot sow.
  Let wheat and tares together grow,
Until the harvest come at last.

THE moon had left the throbbing sea,
　　But dropp'd a trail of light
　　Behind her, as she rose, and he
Clung to that glory lovingly,
　　And wore it through the night.

The smile the sun gave, when he set,
　　Lived long on sky and river;
And in my heart such sweet regret
For my dead love is living yet—
　　God help me, I forgive her.

CHISWICK PRESS:—PRINTED BY WHITTINGHAM AND WILKINS,
TOOKS COURT, CHANCERY LANE.

www.ingramcontent.com/pod-product-compliance
Lightning Source LLC
Chambersburg PA
CBHW060517030726

47498CB00004B/974